THE LIFE AND TIMES OF BARLY BEACH

The little fishing harbour of Barly provides an ideal refuge for recently divorced city-girl, Jenny Sharpe, and her young son Thomas. Over the years, as Jenny and Thomas become absorbed into the close-knit community, Barly comes under threat: not only is it being slowly swallowed up by the encroaching suburbs of the neighbouring seaside resort of Innismouth, it also proves to be an irresistible attraction for greedy property developers who have secretly been buying up land in and around the village.

Intertwined with Jenny's story is that of present-day Barly and its fight against plans to turn it into a giant leisure complex—plans which seem to have every chance of success until they are opposed by the tough, beer-swilling trawlerwoman of Barly Quay.

In her sparkling second novel, Sylvia Murphy cleverly dovetails past and present and casts a cooly ironic eye over the dubious practices of big business and the wheeling and dealing of petty officials looking after their own interests. Against a background of sun and sand, of treacherous tides and near-disasters at sea, *The Life and Times of Barly Beach* is a witty and delightful read.

By the same author:

THE COMPLETE KNOWLEDGE OF SALLY FRY

THE LIFE AND TIMES OF BARLY BEACH

Sylvia Murphy

LONDON
VICTOR GOLLANCZ LTD
1987

First published in Great Britain 1987
by Victor Gollancz Ltd,
14 Henrietta Street, London WC2E 8QJ

© Sylvia Murphy 1987

British Library Cataloguing in Publication Data

Murphy, Sylvia
 The life and times of Barly Beach.
 I. Title
 823'.914[F]   PR6063.U1

ISBN 0-575-03922-1

Printed in Great Britain by
St Edmundsbury Press Ltd, Bury St Edmunds, Suffolk

To David

There are no such places as Barly and Innismouth and all the characters in this tale are figments of the author's imagination. Any resemblance to real people, living or dead, is coincidental.

ONE

Thomas always thought his mother might drown herself, and she did. But that's the end of a long story. On the way there many interesting things happened.

★ ★ ★

Thomas came to Barly with his mother when he was almost too young to remember having lived anywhere else. In later years, when he tried, he could recall a red brick house in a leafy garden near London, but at the time that this story begins his impressions were of a long train journey away from a big city where his mother had cried a great deal.

Strictly speaking it wasn't Barly they came to at first but Innismouth, the small town on the seaward side of the easterly point of the Innis Estuary. Barly was the adjacent village on the river side of the point, taking advantage of the estuary to shelter its little harbour. Later, as Innismouth spread, the two joined together and Barly became an outlying district of the town. With its quaint fishermen's cottages and towering harbour wall it offered the holiday makers different charms from the Edwardian promenade and long sandy beach of Innismouth. But when Thomas and his mother arrived they were simply a small seaside town and a small estuary harbour, linked by a short road across the hill of the point and undisturbed by the effects of motorways and high-speed trains.

Jenny, Thomas's mother, had been there for a holiday years ago with her own mother and her fierce Aunt Patrick Mallory, who had vague aristocratic connections and lived in a flat near Harrods. The holiday had left Jenny with idyllic memories of paddling in the rock pools with her skirt tucked into the elastic of her navy-blue knickers, and being allowed to take off her socks and shoes and walk on the sand, all of which was unladylike and strictly forbidden back home in Kensington. So when, feeling desperate and lonely, she saw an advertisement for cheap off-season weeks in the Marine Hotel, Innismouth, she said to Thomas, "We need a holiday. We'll go to the seaside."

This was exciting. Thomas had been to the seaside before, one day during the summer that had just passed, when his father had gone away for a few days and left his mother with the car, and she had invited the next-door mother and her two children and driven them all to Brighton where they had picnicked on the beach and played in the water and had rides on donkeys and eaten ice creams. So he knew what seasides were all about.

He was surprised that it took a long time for the train to get there. He sat hour after hour on the edge of his seat watching for the water to appear, not noticing that his mother's face was drawn and tense and that occasionally, when she looked up from the book she was reading and glanced at the passing fields and villages, her eyes brimmed with tears.

When he saw Innismouth he was disappointed. For the last hour of the railway journey he had been catching glimpses of a blue and lovely sea as the train wound its way along the coastline. But then they had to wait at a cold, windy station to change on to a smaller train and by the time they alighted from the taxi at the hotel the sea was grey and heavy. Large spots of rain were beginning to fall. There were no donkeys or ice-cream vans and there didn't seem to be any beach. The waves broke right against the huge granite wall across the road from the hotel. They were given a small room at the back and when Thomas asked whether they couldn't have one overlooking the sea, his mother said, "It seems we're not very important people, Thomas." Guests who were paying cheap, off-season bargain rates were obviously an inferior type of person, or perhaps the cut-rate offer was the only way the hotel could fill its third-best rooms.

The first dinner at the hotel was roast pork and cabbage, which Thomas didn't like. All the people in the dining-room seemed quiet and old, and his mother wouldn't let him stay up to watch the cowboy film on the television in the hotel lounge. It was Thomas's turn to cry as he fell asleep cuddling his teddy bear.

But in the morning the sun shone and the falling tide revealed wide stretches of sand and sparkling rock pools. One or two small sailing boats popped out of the river estuary and dashed smartly back and forth along the seafront. Thomas and his mother took off their socks and shoes and played all day, fishing for tiny crabs in the pools and drawing pictures in the sand. They watched the water creeping back towards the town, washing away their pictures, and they found a café that sold ice creams and cups of tea.

By evening they were warm and relaxed, and Jenny plucked up the courage to ask if they couldn't have one of the tables by the window in the dining-room instead of the one they had been allocated near to the service door. The black-skirted waitress sniffed disdainfully and fetched the very superior head waiter, who looked down his nose at them and explained that the tables by the window were reserved for the guests in the more expensive rooms, but that as they were vacant at the moment madam and her son could occupy one, as long as they didn't mind being moved the next day if more important people arrived.

Jenny noticed that the other women in the dining-room were dressed rather more smartly than she had thought to be necessary other than for weddings and Christmas, and they were wearing real jewellery. They all belonged to a couple or a family group and this made her feel uncomfortable at first because it accentuated her sense of being alone in the world with Thomas. She made a great effort on the following evenings, always wearing her single string of pearls or the gold brooch her mother had given her, and trying to compensate with good grooming for her lack of couturier clothes. Although they had to change tables twice during the week, they were not relegated again to the place near the service door.

After a few days Thomas decided that this was a good place to be, because he liked the sand and the water and the fishing boats that tied up alongside the quay in the little harbour at Barly, and his mother seemed to be happier. Jenny realised that she was enjoying herself just on her own with Thomas, and she came to the decision that she didn't need to be part of a family or to compete with the other women in the hotel in order to be happy being a mother. There would be problems, of course, and she ought to ask her aunt about seeing a solicitor when they returned to London, but she knew that somehow she would be able to manage now.

When they sat at breakfast in the bay window, irritating the waitress who wanted to clear up by lingering and watching the tide coming in over the beach, and she said, "This is our last day, Thomas," he knew that he didn't want to go away.

"I don't want to go home," he said. "I like it here, Mum. Can't we stay?"

"We can't afford another week."

"I don't mean another week. I mean for ever."

"That's a long time."

"It's a nice place."

Jenny could only agree with him. Was there any need for them to go anywhere else? After breakfast she bought a local paper and began to make enquiries about a place to rent for the winter.

By the following afternoon they had found what they needed, one of four caravans in a field overlooking the estuary, holiday lets going cheap for the winter to keep them warm and dry.

THE LIFE AND TIMES OF BARLY BEACH

The caravans and the field belonged to Joshua Brown, a wealthy farmer who, Jenny was told, owned most of the land between Barly and the encroaching outskirts of Innismouth. She later learned that he was the great-grandson of a Squire Jeffery Brown, the man mainly responsible for the founding of Innismouth, and this made him one of Barly's more important people. Like Squire Jeffery, who had seen the potential of a few holiday villas and a luxury hotel when the railway had sent a branch line to Barly for the fish trade, and had sold off some of his seaside land for development, Joshua never missed an opportunity to make money. For years he had encouraged his wife Rosie to take paying guests in the farmhouse for summer holidays and the farm became known amongst a select circle of nice families who liked the peace and quiet. When their friends began bringing tents and touring caravans and asking if they could use one of the fields for camping, Joshua kindly allowed them in and charged them small sums of money, which he began to invest in caravans of his own that were parked in the field and let out for rather larger sums.

Rosie didn't consider that these caravans were suitable for living in during the winter, up on the exposed hillside, but Joshua insisted that as long as people were willing to pay he was willing to let and nobody had complained, though this may have been due to the fact that the people who lived in the caravans during the winter months had nowhere else to go.

Jenny had no thoughts of anything but gratitude when she and Thomas moved their few possessions into the caravan. At last, for a few months, she was relieved of the pressure that had driven her here in the first place. The respite would give her time to think, to sort out what to do with her life.

Thomas was so excited that he found it quite difficult to behave himself for a while.

Once they had settled in they found the caravan very cosy and congenial. They had a paraffin stove, which Thomas was careful not to go near, and a little black-and-white television set which would flicker on and off when the gales screamed in from the ocean and buffeted the aerial. Their neighbours were an elderly couple who shouted at each other a lot and a young woman called Myra, a sociology lecturer from London who had taken a year off to write a book and who popped in for cups of tea several times a day. She would say she'd called in for a chat when the writing was difficult, or to see if Jenny wanted anything at the shop, but cleverly she seemed able to plan her visits to coincide almost exactly with the times when Jenny was about to put the kettle on, or had just brewed a pot.

Writing must give her a terrible thirst, Jenny thought, as Myra replenished her cup for the third time from an almost empty pot, and talked about the oppression of women by society and something she called "gender role definition". When Jenny asked for an expalanation of what she meant it turned out to be what Jenny had always imagined to be the natural way of dividing life's chores between men and women. According to Myra this was not natural at all but dictated by men so that women had the more menial work to do. Jenny made the mistake of disagreeing and saying that she didn't think it mattered much how it was divided up, and by whom, as long as everyone had something unpleasant and something pleasant to do. She realised as she was speaking that she ought to have kept quiet and just listened with admiring attention. Myra made a strange harrumphing noise and stomped out and banged the door.

"Why is she so angry?" Thomas asked. "Doesn't she like us any more?"

"She'll be back," said Jenny, "next time I boil the kettle."

Thus Thomas and Jenny settled down to spend their first winter in Barly and to become acquainted with the people there. Every now and again, instead of a bedtime story, Thomas liked to count up how many new friends they had, and Jenny would add little mental notes of her own as he ticked them off on small fingers that were just beginning to lose their baby chubbiness.

There was Myra with her cropped hair and dungarees and strange ideas; Joshua, wiry and energetic like one of his sheepdogs, with a gleam of imagination in his eyes; Rosie, by contrast, about as energetic and imaginative as one of the sheep; Mrs Sing at the shop, who was gentle and sprightly with long greying hair tied into a bunch at the back of her neck like a young girl's. She was very kind to Thomas, and Jenny felt an affinity from her which she understood when Rosie told her that Mrs Sing had run the shop and brought up two children on her own since her husband had left twenty years ago, to sail around the world with a friend, and had never been heard of again. Then there were the rambling, complicated families of the Bakers and the Dogs who owned the fishing boats and lived in the cottages on the quayside, and Thomas often fell asleep before he had counted all of them—but they come later in the story.

★ ★ ★

A public meeting has been arranged in the Royal Hall for the residents of Innismouth and Barly to express their feelings about the new development plan for Barly Beach. It is to be presided over by James Box, senior partner of the firm of Box and Baffle, Solicitors, and Chairman of the Town Council. It is to his advantage, in more ways than one, for the development plan to be approved and implemented, but he cannot give any indication of this. He has to be seen to be acting in the public interest first and because of this the motions of consultation are most important.

James Box takes his public image very seriously. He has lived in Innismouth all his life, apart from the time when his parents sent him to boarding school to benefit from a superior type of education. He didn't shine academically and only just gained a place at university where he was one of the few students who managed to leave without a degree. He was only able to attain the staus of solicitor because his father took him on in the family firm as soon as he left university and was prepared to support him for several years whilst he struggled to study for the law exams, which he regularly failed. Finally, at the age of twenty-nine, he was made a full partner in the firm without the necessary qualifications, but he was so inept at handling even the more straightforward of the clients' affairs that his father suggested he should take an interest in local politics. Encouraged by public apathy he found no difficulty in being elected on to the Town Council and his father then had an excuse to take on another, brighter, junior partner, Paul Baffle, who handled most of the legal business while James concentrated on his public work, which entailed joining a great many local clubs and associations and spending much of his time at meetings or in the bars of those clubs.

By the time he is fifty and is flabby, greying and posy faced, he has become a County Councillor as well as Chairman of the Town Council, and the arrangement whereby Baffle does all the work in the firm and Box arranges public matters has worked very well for some twenty years or so. Box and Baffle is the most respected firm of solicitors in town and James Box is a very important public figure, organising the lives of his electorate in a way most beneficial to all—all those who matter, anyway.

The plans for the redevelopment of Barly and the small island in the mouth of the estuary have been available for inspection in the Town Hall at Innismouth for some months. A few people have been in and asked to see them but most have been content to be informed by the reports in the *Innismouth Herald*. Most of the reactions have been favourable. The once separate village of Barly has long since been swallowed up by the upstart Edwardian seaside town of Innismouth as it has crept unchecked up the hills inland and across the point that marks the end of the estuary and the beginning of the open sea. Whilst remaining a quaint and undeveloped community within the town because of its origins as a fishing harbour Barly is now, in the eyes of the most important residents of Innismouth, who are in a position to make big decisions, rather scruffy. Development will be a good thing. It will bring more money.

Wearing his well-pressed and very neutral council chairman's suit, with a plain blue tie, James Box sits in the central chair at the trestle-table that has been set up on the platform of the Royal Hall. He leans back, a pose calculated to express confidence, and talks to the man sitting beside him, the Town Council Treasurer, watching with half an eye the trickle of little old ladies, hoteliers, and Barly residents coming into the hall, scraping and shuffling the folding wooden chairs as they arrange themselves in appropriate groups to gossip with their neighbours. He can identify the Barly residents because they always manage to look as down-at-heel as their environment. They do not seem to understand the concept of changing into clothes appropriate for the occasion after they have finished work.

Although the hall will seat two hundred people in comfort, the caretaker has been told to put out only a hundred chairs and the organisers are doubtful that these will be filled. Public meetings do not attract much attention, especially when they have been carefully timed to coincide with an important football match on the television.

Other people arrive to take up the seats on the platform: the architect who has prepared the plans, the Town Clerk of Innismouth, and a representative of the Black Corproation who are financing the development and who own much of the land on which it will be situated. James Box does not know the name of this representative. He has advised his friend Rufus Black, Chairman and Senior Executive of the Corporation, to keep a low profile at this stage.

Two people enter the hall who do not immediately sit down with the others but come to the top table, clutching a sheaf of papers. One is an elderly, thickset man with snowy hair, gnarled hands, and the leathered, ruddy complexion that comes from years of exposure to salt winds and sunshine. He is dressed in a heavy white roll-necked sweater, faded corduroys, a salt-stained donkey jacket, and rubber boots. The other is a woman, or so it would seem from her greying hair which is longer than a man's and permed into a wild frizz that shows no sign of having been combed for some time. She is also wind-tanned and thickset and it is quite difficult to detet the roundness of a woman's breasts beneath her sweater and jacket. On close inspection, which few people accord her, she is obviously rather younger than her companion, just about young enough to be his daughter, perhaps.

It is the woman who places the sheaf of papers, curled at the edges and held together with a bulldog clip, on the table in front of James Box.

"Our petition," she says curtly, "against this plan." The old man with her nods.

James Box leans forwards, catching a whiff of fish. "Whose petition?" he asks politely.

"Ours. From Barly. Seven hundred signatures. We don't want none of it, and anyway it won't work." The old man nods again.

"Thank you," says the Chairman, taking up the petition. "We will consider your views, along with everyone else's of course. If you will kindly take your seats we can proceed." As the couple move away towards some vacant chairs he riffles through the petition, glancing cursorily at some of the signatures.

"Are there seven hundred people in Barly?" asks the Town Clerk anxiously.

"I doubt it," replies James Box. "Not who can write their names, anyway."

"What shall we do about it?"

"Ignore it. It isn't constitutional."

The meeting is opened by a long speech from the Chairman explaining the basic principles of the plan: to extend Barly Harbour and turn it into a yachting marina; to build flats and hotels from Barly Quay up the hillside overlooking the estuary; to build a causeway across the underwater sandbar to the island in the mouth of the estuary; and to build a leisure complex on the island. He also explains the benefits in terms of the attractions that will be provided for visiting yachtsmen, the further influx of tourists spending their money in the town, the enhancement of the environment in general with the tidying up of the Barly side of the town. All this takes a long time and is very boring for the listeners who are only there because they know about it already. Almost before he has finished hands are being raised in the audience. He has to accept questions from the floor, he knows, but he has learned to be selective about whose hands he notices. Time after time he points to another questioner as the pair who presented the petition draw breath and raise their arms.

Yes, the people whose homes are to be demolished will be given special consideration for council housing, or be allowed to buy flats in the new development at preferential prices.

Yes, local people will be given first options to take up the new business premises that will be made available.

Yes, the architect's engineers have made a study of the effects of the new development on the tidal flow, and there should be no problems.

Yes, once Barly Beach is closed there will be public access to the estuary by way of a promenade and there will be slipways for launching small boats in the vicinity of the Sailing Club.

Finally he glances at his watch and says, "Well, I know the caretaker will be wanting to close up now. We've had a good cross-section of views here and I think the council has gained a fair idea of what the public feels about the development."

But he's too late. The fishy-smelling woman leaps to her feet. "Just a minute! You've ignored us! You can't just take away our homes and our living like that! How're we to land our fish in a posh marina? How can we live in some holiday flat when we've had our cottages on the quay for years? How can we bring our boats in through your causeway? You're ignoring the fishermen! You're raping our environment!"

There are a few rumblings of "Aye, that's right," but the general reaction is a snigger running through the hall. The combination of the angry woman's unfeminine appearance and her reference to rape is too much for the collective imagination.

"Madam," says James Box calmly, "If you wish to oppose the plan you may do so by expressing your views to your local Councillor."

"Just so!" she shouts. "You're my bloody Councillor and I'm bloody telling you!"

"And I am listening. But this is a democracy and the views of the majority will prevail in the end."

"Not over my home, they won't!" But she subsides, being pulled back into her chair by the old man beside her who mutters something in her ear.

As the hall clears the representative of the Black Corporation leans across and asks James Box, "Who is that person?"

THE LIFE AND TIMES OF BARLY BEACH

"Mrs Baker, a local fisherman's widow. Since her husband died she's run a trawler on her own. She's one of these colourful characters who scrapes a living from the fishing and spends most of it on drink. There's always one of them about and they're easy to deal with. All noise. Soon get out of the way when they see a bit of money."

The first discussion of the Barly Development plan in the Innismouth Town Council causes some unprecedented disturbance. To begin with, the usher has to bring in several extra chairs to the small gallery set aside for the public, and then, as yet more of the residents of Barly troop in, he has to leave the doors open to the entrance hall and allow them to sit there. He would have excluded those who came late but on being confronted by Mrs Baker, who says in no uncertain terms that they all have a right to be there and they will hold up the meeting if places can't be found for them, he allows them to stay. He knows that Mrs Baker is not a woman to be put to inconvenience, and he notices that as the Town Councillors file silently into the chamber from their anteroom several of them turn a little pale at the sight of the delegation and its leader. One or two exchange glances and raise their eyebrows superciliously. Those who know better lower their heads into their hands and mumble their way into the agenda.

When they come to the Barly Development item, Chairman Box makes a brisk and important little speech about the benefits to Innismouth and Barly of allowing the development to take place as planned and in the far corner three reporters eagerly scribble in their pads. Most of the land required is already owned by the corporation who have applied for planning permission, he says, and the Committee is recommending that the Council pass the plans subject to compulsory purchase of a few remaining properties in Barly and the closing of the quay and harbour to public commercial traffic. To judge by comments received from members of the public, he says, the overwhelming majority are in favour of this development, which will put the town of Innismouth well and truly on the tourist map, in a position to compete with places like Torbay and Newquay. He sits down and invites comments or questions from members of the

Council. Heads around the table shake gently and he says in that case they'll take a vote.

"What about our comments and questions?" comes a voice from the front row of the public gallery. "What about us? It's our bloody place you're talking about, not Innismouth! It's our boats you're going to put out of business and our beach you're going to build your bloody funfair on!"

By the time she's finished Mrs Baker is on her feet, leaning across the rail that separates her from the Councillors. Several voices mutter in agreement behind her and the public gives a round of applause.

The Chairman's voice is confidently steady as he says, "May I remind members of the public that this is not the place to express their opinions. You should have informed your councillors earlier of your views. You are here to listen only. Any further disturbance will cause you to be removed from the chamber."

The usher looks doubtful at this and he has the foresight to leave the chamber and come back accompanied by a solitary policeman who has volunteered to earn some quiet overtime policing the meeting. The sight of the policeman quietens all but Mrs Baker who continues to shout, "We have told our bloody Councillors our views, Mr Bloody Bumblebox! We have and they take no notice! That's because they're all in that development company's pockets, same as you! Bloody crooks, the lot of you!"

Councillor Box turns to the usher and the policeman and says, "Kindly remove that woman from the chamber."

The policeman says a quiet word to the usher, who walks over and says a quiet word to the Chairman, who nods and says, "I declare this meeting suspended." The Councillors breathe a collective sigh of relief and gather up their papers and file hastily into their anteroom, tripping over chairs and each other's heels in order to be out of the way as soon as possible. The residents of Barly, not quite sure whether they've scored a victory or not, rumble out of the front door and go home.

★ ★ ★

When Thomas and Jenny came to Barly it was before the amusement arcade and the funfair and any talk of the new development with the marina and the luxury flats. She was a slim young woman of medium height with anxious eyes and dark, backcombed hair, who wore mostly oversized sweaters and tapered slacks with bands under her feet to keep the line neat, as was the fashion then. He was a small, tidy boy with reddish cropped hair and sturdy dimpled knees above his Marks and Spencer socks and Clarks sandals. At first they were unnoticed among the rather superior families who stayed in the Marine Hotel, but when they moved into one of Joshua Brown's caravans people began to talk about them and wish them the time of day as they walked along the beach or fetched their shopping from Mrs Sing's General Store by the harbour. The people of Barly were cautious with strangers but they were secretly pleased when anyone liked their village enough to want to stay there permanently. So they were welcoming in a distant kind of way, giving the newcomers a chance.

Thomas, with his open smiling face and his frank manner of conversation, was easy to get along with but they found his mother rather closed and secretive, giving away little of herself. They speculated and swapped stories of a broken marriage, or an illegitimate child unwisely kept, none of which Jenny ever confirmed or denied. They construed her reticence, coupled with a precise Home Counties accent of which she was unaware, as being stuck-up. They muttered about her being born with a silver spoon in her mouth and having come down in the world, which was partially true except that it was Thomas's grandmother who had come down in the world and had tried to prepare her daughter Jenny for a standard of living to which she had no hope of becoming accustomed. Her final failure had been to die while Jenny was still a schoolgirl, thus ensuring an early and ill-judged marriage.

Jenny had left her small and undistinguished boarding school with no qualifications other than the skills needed to be a correct and charming hostess. She had been led by the spinster headmistress to believe that these skills, plus certain standards of grooming and sexual morality never made explicit, were all that was needed to ensure the love of a good man and thus fulfil herself as the mother of a large family.

Some of the other girls at school, from more secure and liberated homes, expressed scorn at this view of their future. But Jenny was enough of a realist to see that she could never hope to earn sufficient money to provide for herself comfortably and marriage seemed the only sensible ambition in the circumstances.

"But you wouldn't marry for money, would you?" one of her friends hissed across the darkened dormitory during one of those frequent discussions about that most interesting of topics, future husbands. "How sordid!"

"Of course not!" Jenny hissed back. "But how much more convenient it would be if one fell in love with a wealthy man!"

Before too long, of course, she did fall in love, with the elder brother of one of her school-friends who invited her to stay for the summer after they left. Later, equipped with the clear perspective of hindsight, she decided that she had allowed herself to be emotionally seduced by his blond good looks and well-cut suits, and the fact that he was something up-and-coming in the city, but at the time she thought it was love. Knowing that a wife with social accomplishments would be an asset he bought her an engagement ring and a pretty house. Within weeks of being married she was pregnant with Thomas because there didn't seem to be any point in not starting that large family right away. It never occurred to her that she had not discussed the size or timing of this family with her husband. Indeed they had never discussed anything more important than the colour of the bedroom curtains and the kitchen tiles.

She suffered considerably and unexpectedly before and during Thomas's birth, which led her to modify her view of herself as the mother of a large brood. Then, being unable to have sex without pain for some months and needing a small operation eventually to put matters right, she naturally thought that her husband would endure celibacy out of respect for her needs. It came as a shock to find out that he was having an affair with his secretary. Her sense of failure was acute. Sad and bewildered she played the role of a good wife wronged for three years before he left her altogether, telling her he could only afford to pay her an allowance for Thomas, not herself, and she must work for her living. Eventually he sold the house they lived in so that he could afford to buy a bigger and smarter one for his new wife, and Jenny took Thomas to stay with her only living relative, her Aunt Patrick in Knightsbridge. Aunt Patrick was sympathetic but as she disliked children intensely the atmosphere was uncomfortable so after a few weeks Jenny and Thomas came to Barly.

"Why is it called Barly?" Thomas asked. "There isn't any barley sugar here, except in Mrs Sing's shop."

"I don't know," Jenny replied with scant attention as they tramped their way along the cliff top, watching the brief October sun rolling towards a misty horizon and hearing the breakers crashing on the rocks below them. Jenny was frightened of the wind and the sea and she came up here for walks because her fear made her forget her sorrow and humiliation.

Slowly she began to feel better about her failure as she talked to Myra, who congratulated her on liberating herself from marriage and lent her books to read and told her amazing things about her libido and her psyche, neither of which she knew she possessed until then. She decided that she ought to educate herself to do something to earn a proper living and support Thomas so she sent for a prospectus and enrolled on an Arts Foundation Course with the Open University. When she heard she had been accepted as a student she made a special trip to the nearby large town of Halmouth to sell her engagement ring to pay the course fee and buy her books.

"Why do you need all those books?" Thomas asked, handling them carefully as Jenny unpacked them.

"So that I can understand the world," Jenny said. "Education is important, you know. It stops you making mistakes."

Thomas thought about this. He knew that because he was five now he had to go to school after Christmas, down the hill in Barly. They had already been to see the teacher who had smiled brightly and said how pleased she would be to have him there. But then he had heard her say to his mother that it was a pity they weren't more settled because insecurity made it difficult for children to learn.

"What does being settled mean?" he asked Jenny.

"Problems," Jenny replied, thinking of the red brick house and the regular routine of her husband going out each morning and returning each evening, never telling her what he had been doing in between.

"But I want to learn to read and the teacher said I might not if I'm not settled."

"Just do your work and be good," Jenny said. "If I can learn here then you can."

So in the evenings they sat each side of the wobbly table, Thomas practising his letters and learning his word cards and Jenny writing long assignments that she stuffed into brown envelopes and posted on the way to school in the mornings.

"Why is it called Barly here?" Thomas asked one of the fishermen who was sitting on the quay mending a big net. He had run ahead of Jenny as they walked back from school. There was a quicker way home to the caravan but Thomas liked to look at the boats and Jenny liked to climb up from the harbour through the fields. From the path they could see a little wooded island in the mouth of the estuary and look out over the tidal reaches of the River Innis, sometimes a broad expanse of sand and mud flats, sometimes brimming with grey water, according to the state of the tide.

"Someone's pulled the plug out today," Thomas would say when the tide had ebbed and the river was a solitary channel winding between the exposed flats. Of course he wanted to know why it was different every day, so they took books out of the library in Innismouth and more or less worked the system out for themselves—how there were twelve hours and a bit between every high tide, and how twice a month the high tides were extra high, which were called springs, and twice a month they were not so high at high tide and not so low at low tide, which were called neaps. It was all organised by the moon, springs on a full and a new moon and neaps at half-moon, which Thomas thought was terribly clever. He was glad he knew about it because it helped him to understand some of the things the fishermen were saying at times.

Jenny wasn't too happy when Thomas stopped to talk to the men. There were usually six of them, two older men and a gang of younger ones who looked as though they might be sons or nephews. Between them they worked three small trawlers, all that was left of Barly's fishing fleet by that time. They looked gruff and forbidding, and they would often stare at her when she passed and make remarks to one another and laugh, which made her afraid of them. But when they sat on the quay smoking or working on their fishing gear Thomas approached them readily to ask questions, so she came close but hung back, listening to their answers.

"Barly?" One of the older men scratched his head. "Well now, 'tus Barly because it lies beside the bar, I think."

"The bar?"

"Out there." He pointed to the stretch of water between the harbour wall and the island. "There's a sand-bar just beneath the water there. Tide's up now but you'll see how the breakers crash over it at low tide, and at low springs it shows above the water. You got to know it to get safely in and out of here but that's what keeps us sheltered from the big ocean swells, see. It's our friend and our enemy, like, depending."

"Can I have a go in one of your boats one day?" Thomas asked.

The other older man answered, "Better ask your mum, little fellow." He shot a glance and a wink towards Jenny which was almost friendly and made her feel for the first time that these were not hostile people. "Perhaps she'd like to come too."

"Oh no," Thomas said firmly. "She wouldn't. She's frightened of the water."

"So are we all. But we go on it, not in it."

"If you let me come," Thomas said, "I think I could be helpful, holding things and keeping a lookout."

"When the weather's better we'll see. Now run along, your mum's waiting." As Thomas turned away the man smiled again and gave Jenny a friendly wave. She made up her mind that next time they passed that way she would stop and talk as well, so as not to appear standoffish.

In fact their next meeting was not quite so regular because it was the two older men, Abel Baker and Charlie Dog, who answered Thomas's cries and pulled Jenny out of the water when she fell off the path on the seaward side of the harbour wall. It was a narrow path, slippery with seaweed, that led around to the rocky point at low tide but was covered at high tide. Jenny and Thomas were racing along it dodging the surges of the incoming tide, and Jenny slipped on a piece of seaweed; before she could pick herself up a wave swept her into the cold water. They were all sure she was dead by the time they dragged her slender body on to the beach but someone pumped at her chest and someone else brought blankets and they kept her breathing until the ambulance arrived. Abel Baker took Thomas into his warm cottage and Mrs Baker, a thin, jolly woman, gave him tea while her husband changed into dry clothes and told her what had happened.

"We thought she was a gonner," he said, shaking his head. "We haven't had a drowning here all year."

"You must take care," Sarah Baker said to Thomas. "You look after your mum. The water's dangerous."

TWO

When summer came again they had to leave the caravan. They stayed as long as they could but Joshua told them firmly that it was let for holidays from the middle of May and they would have to be out by then. Myra went to London with her finished book, optimistic that it was just what the world was waiting for—the female half anyway. Jenny was not so sure that many of them would be able to understand it. The angry couple packed up and went off one day without telling anyone where they were going, which wasn't surprising considering that they owed the Browns two months' rent. Jenny asked around in Innismouth and Barly but although people were sympathetic, their sympathy didn't extend to letting anything less than the price they would get from holiday visitors and she couldn't afford that.

"It's not that they don't want you," said Nora Dog, folding her plump arms across her overflowing bosom. "But there's always people looking at this time of year and if they gives in to one it makes it difficult to refuse others, see?"

"We'd have you here, dear," said Sarah Baker, "if there

was room." But there clearly wasn't. The tiny cottages already seemed overfull with large men and wet sea-boots and oilskins. Jenny told Thomas they would have to go back to London for the summer and stay with Aunt Patrick.

Neither of them liked that idea. They had grown used to Barly and the estuary and become happy there. After Jenny's accident they had often been invited to tea by Sarah or Nora and they were on friendly terms with all the men in the two families, who would pat Thomas on the head and sometimes give him little newspaper parcels of fresh fish. They no longer just shopped at Mrs Sing's but lingered and gossiped about what was going on around the place, or what the newspapers had to say that day.

"We'll come back," Jenny assured Thomas. "We'll book the caravan again for next winter and come back."

"But I want to stay for the summer," Thomas said. "Why don't we go and live on the island?" They often stood on the hillside or on the beach, looking across at the little island in the estuary with its few trees and its mass of thick grasses and bushes. They made up stories about it and people who might live there.

"Nobody can really live on the island, darling," Jenny said absently, looking up from the D. H. Lawrence novel she was reading for her course and which she was finding rather disturbing, with its dark sexual images. "There are no houses."

"We could take a tent." Thomas had watched people camping in the field alongside them since Easter and it looked all right to him.

"There isn't any drinking water."

"We could fetch it in a boat."

"Well, that's it. We don't have a boat to get there."

"Someone would give us a lift."

"Thomas darling, it just isn't practical. Nobody can live on tne island." She always said "darling" when she wanted to insist on something and Thomas knew he ought to agree with her, but he very badly didn't want to go to London and he was sure his mother felt the same.

"Some people are living there now."

"Only in those stories we make up."

"No, real people. I saw them. They've got a boat and they came yesterday to get some shopping and pick up someone. Mrs Sing says they're happies."

Unable to concentrate on her book because of Thomas's conversation, Jenny glanced up out of the caravan window and across the estuary and she saw a thin wisp of camp fire smoke rising from amongst the trees on the island. Happies? Did he mean hippies? Those strange love-and-flowers people who had attracted the attention of the newspapers in the last couple of years? The island did seem like the sort of place they might settle, where nobody could get at them. But would they be allowed to stay there? Wouldn't the authorities do something about it?

Every day one or two more of them arrived and Thomas and Jenny watched them waiting on Barly Beach with their belongings until a small wooden boat with a noisy, spluttering outboard motor came across to fetch them.

"I won't be able to do my assignments," Jenny said.

"Yes you will. I'll make you a little wooden table to write on and you can post them when someone comes across to get food and water."

"You won't be able to go to school."

"I'll do my lessons every day, I promise. I can already read. I'm two books ahead of some of the others in the class."

"We can't afford to buy a tent."

"Mrs Sing says she has a tent in her loft that her son used to use. She says we can borrow it."

Jenny looked at his anxious face and thought how awful London would be after Barly. It'll only be for a few weeks, if that, she thought. It'll make him happy. He'll soon get fed up with it and then we can sort out something more permanent.

So, on the day they had to move out of the caravan, she packed as much as she could into two old rucksacks Myra had given her and asked Joshua if she could leave a case of belongings in one of his storerooms. She went to the shop to collect some food and the tent.

"It's all ready," said Mrs Sing. "One of the lads got it out of the loft yesterday."

"We're going on a little camping holiday."
"Over to the island, I hear."
"Staying with the happies," put in Thomas.
"Yes. Do you think it will be all right?" Jenny blushed anxiously. She knew that hippies didn't have a very favourable reputation and it would be dreadful to offend Mrs Sing after she had been so kind and friendly.
"Oh yes. They're a rum lot, camping out like kids, but they don't bother no one. Few of them comes down every year. You'll be all right. And the little lad will enjoy it."
They took their luggage, together with a five-gallon water container, also loaned by Mrs Sing, down to the beach where Thomas assured Jenny someone would soon pick them up. Before long the little boat put out from the island and landed alongside them. It was driven by a young man with long black hair and a beard, wearing jeans and a flowered shirt and looking more like Jesus Christ than a ferryman.
"You're ready at last," he said as he lifted their bags aboard.
"Is it all right? Are we allowed?"
"Anyone can join. We were wondering why you were taking so long."
"You've been expecting us?"
"Oh yes. Your little fellow told us last week that you'd be coming."
The ride across the choppy water in the overloaded ferryboat was the first time Thomas and his mother had been afloat. Thomas knelt in the bows, his eager face turned towards the approaching island, the wind blowing his hair back, blissfully unaware that he was in imminent danger of being deposited in the water if the boat rolled. Jenny sat amidships clutching the thwart she was sitting on, her heart sinking every time the motor, which seemed no more adequate than an egg whisk, spluttered and threatened to stop.
The boatman seemed as anxious as she was, muttering to himself each time the motor changed its pitch. He was constantly twiddling the little knobs on the engine which appeared to Jenny to be causing more problems than it

cured, not least because every time his attention turned from the course he was steering to the adjustments he was making, the boat veered in a wide snakelike motion through the water which increased its instability.

"I don't usually do this job," the man said. "I'm not really familiar with the controls."

Jenny could see that this was true and she had difficulty in remembering why it had seemed like a good idea to make this journey. It was something Thomas had organised, wasn't it? And wasn't she the one who was supposed to be in charge?

Memories returned of the cold waters closing over her head on the day the trawlermen had rescued her and she was quite sure that if ever she reached the island safely there would never be any good reason to return to the mainland.

★ ★ ★

Around the kitchen table inside a cottage on Barly Quay where members of the Baker family have lived for the last two hundred years, the present Mrs Baker is holding a council of war. Abel's two sons, Sam and Victor, are there and Sam's wife, Chrissie; so is Charlie Dog and his son, Jim. Thomas Sharpe, the boat-builder, is sitting on a high stool against the wall, quiet and serious and keeping in the background as he usually does. Old Mrs Sing from the shop sits across the table from Mrs Baker. All these people make the room very crowded.

The focus of their attention is a report in the *Innismouth Herald* that the council has unanimously passed the plans put forward by the Black Corporation for the redevelopment of Barly. There is a plan and a sketch showing an extended harbour wall enclosing a smart yacht marina with shops and restaurants around it, a causeway of piles across the bar to the island, an entertainments complex on the island with more shops and restaurants and a sports hall, and ranks of Mediterranean-style flats on the quay in place of the cottages and Mrs Sing's shop. It all looks very nice, as Mrs Sing comments, but it isn't Barly. The only mention of the protest at the council meeting is, "After a brief disturbance by a minority of die-hard opponents . . ."

"Brief disturbance!" exclaims Mrs Baker. "We closed their bloody meeting, didn't we?"

"Seems we didn't," says Charlie. "They just carried it on in another room."

"'Tisn't legal. Can't be."

"They done it," says Charlie, puffing on his pipe. "Thing is, what do we do now? Seems they got us beat. Everyone else has sold out, bar us."

Sam and Victor exchange glances and Sam says, "I think we should take their money and use it to replace our boats. They've promised we'll still have our pleasure trip concessions and with new and bigger boats we can take people further down the coast and improve the business."

"I don't want to hear none of that," Charlie growls. "Abe would turn in his grave. We stick together or nothing."

"We'll all be better off selling out," says Thomas Sharpe, "but I don't think we should. What they're going to do will destroy the place."

"Can't stand in the way of progress," says Sam.

Victor nods. "It's going to go anyway. We're wasting our time."

"They can't do anything," says Mrs Baker firmly. "For all their fine plans they can't do a thing while we're in these cottages working our boats from the quay. They got to summon us and go to High Court. It'll take them years."

"But they'll win in the end, with their money," Victor insists, "so why bother?"

Nobody answers that, but they all know why. Barly is their home.

Meanwhile, in a smart solicitor's office not very far away, another conversation is going on that is concerned with the future of Barly. James Box shuffles his feet impatiently while the two younger solicitors in front of him talk on and on, explaining the case point by point and laying each document in front of him as they refer to it. He is impatient because he knows all this already. He has delegated to them the task of dealing with the matter so that he need not be further involved and they are doing it badly. He is impatient because he promised the party who is paying him that the matter would be cleared up weeks ago and he is now under pressure to deliver on that promise.

James Box has a name to live up to and bungled cases do that name no good.

"I can't see the problem," he says at last. "Everyone else has either accepted our cash offer or had their leases terminated. Why can't the same be done with Mrs Baker?"

"She's in a key position, sir, and she knows it, being both a trawler operator and owning two of the cottages on the quay, right in the centre of the area to be developed."

"What's she holding out for? More money? You haven't offered her enough."

"We've been to the ceiling we're allowed and she won't budge."

"What does she want, then?"

"She says she wants to carry on with her trawling. She claims George the Fourth granted irrevocable rights to all fishermen to use the quay and inhabit the cottages in perpetuity."

"And what do you think?"

They glance from one to the other, crisp and pink and uncomfortable. James Box is aware of their discomfort and despises them because they show it. When he was young and eager to impress he would never have shown any colleague or client that he felt uneasy.

"We think she has a case. There is a charter."

"Well I think you've missed an important point. This charter refers to fishermen, does it not?" They nod in unison. "This trawler owner who stands in the way of the Barly development is not a fisherman. She is a woman. She has no case."

There is a moment's silence then one of the young men clears his throat. "With respect sir, we believe she has. These are the 1980s. We have the Equal Opportunities Commission to contend with."

James Box feels his anger rising but he smiles his slow, superior smile which always stands him in good stead on such occasions. "Equal Opportunities Commission? A crowd of hysterical, frustrated women! Nobody takes them seriously." He notes with satisfaction the worried glance that passes between the two young men. He is James Box and they are nothing yet, and they know it. "Offer her more money, just to show generosity, then enforce the compulsory purchase order."

"We can't offer her more without sanction from the Council Treasurer."

"He will sanction whatever sum I tell him has been agreed. Go up another ten thousand if need be. But don't come back and tell me the matter isn't settled."

Another worried glance. "With respect, sir . . ."

"Yes, yes?" "With respect" automatically means without respect, coming from juniors, and these two have demurred enough already.

"We think that if she stands her ground it may come to a public enquiry."

"That must not be allowed to happen. Important interests are at stake for the future of the town. She's only a village woman, and a drunkard from all accounts. She can't have much education. Just tell her firmly that a woman cannot be a trawlerman. Put it in a formally worded letter. She'll understand."

★ ★ ★

Life on Happy Island was far more organised than Jenny had expected. She needn't have brought her container of fresh water because there was a crude but effective solar still that supplied enough for cooking and drinking. Every day someone caught some fish and fresh vegetables were supplied by a succession of bean-sprouting pots. When the tide was high enough to form a shallow lagoon on the side of the island that faced across the river they bathed and washed their clothes. People only went ashore to collect letters and cheques sent by indulgent parents, with which they bought a few luxuries like shampoo and cider.

Thomas was pleased to discover that there were three other children on the island because somehow he had imagined that it would be all grown-ups. The children were two girls and a boy, all a little older than him, and they lived in a house in a tree without anyone ever telling them to come down at once, or to be careful. Thomas took up his sleeping bag and joined them there. Being so high up made the grown-ups look quite small, which was very satisfactory.

Never before had Jenny been amongst a group of people so lacking in anxiety and urgency. There were twelve of them altogether, plus the children, and they spent their days reading, talking or swimming, or just lying around making love with a lack of inhibition that embarrassed Jenny at first. Those who wanted to fished and cooked but there were never any complaints about those who did no work at all.

At first Jenny set aside a few hours every day to do her Open University work and she even completed and posted an assignment. Then she noticed that Lionel, the man who had collected them from the beach, looked at her with dark, burning eyes just like the men D. H. Lawrence had written about, and she found herself giving him more attention than her books. Her interest grew as he talked of nature and freedom and told her to lie back and love and be loved, which she did. This combination of Lionel's resemblance to her visualisation of a D. H. Lawrence hero, and the relaxed situation they were living in, led to her first taste of sexual satisfaction and she realised at last what had been missing from her marriage to Thomas's father. He had always left her feeling on the brink of excitement and then told her it was her fault that she was no good in bed.

She thought that at last she had come to understand the nature of sexual love and she allowed herself to become obsessed by Lionel, going with him everywhere, swimming naked in the moonlight, combing his flowing hair and beard, laundering and mending his clothes. Knowing that all this was not very much in accordance with what Myra had been writing and talking about all winter, Jenny felt a pang of doubt that hung like a question mark at the back of her mind but she was able to tell herself that her present life was fulfilling and natural. Lionel didn't ask her to do things for him, she did them because she wanted to. She tried to discuss Myra's ideas with Lionel, who laughed.

"You are free," he said. "There are no formal bonds between us. You can go to someone else or leave the island whenever you please."

"Of course," Jenny murmured. "But I love you."

THE LIFE AND TIMES OF BARLY BEACH

The gaps between her working days grew more frequent and she fell behind with her next assignment. The week she had booked for summer school approached and passed by. She could have easily arranged for Thomas to stay on the island to be looked after, and gone ashore in the boat, but it didn't see important any more.

Thomas watched his mother dallying in Lionel's arms and he stopped worrying that she might suddenly say they had to go. He himself went everywhere with Silver, a golden-limbed girl with long brown hair, nearly two years older than him, who held his hand and kissed him and told him stories about a wonderful place called India where she said she had been born.

Jenny let her hair grow long and wore a caftan and sandals and a string of wooden beads Lionel gave her. She became thinner than ever and her once anxious eyes became calm and dreamy. She smiled often and fondly on Thomas and hoped that it wouldn't affect his education too much if she didn't insist that he practise his reading every day. She helped him learn to swim and watched him climbing trees and fishing and playing endless imaginary adventures with Silver and the other children. She made sure that he was warm and fed but it often seemed that he only really needed her if he had hurt himself, or thought up a question that was too difficult for other people to answer.

"In the winter can we go to India with Silver and her mum?" he asked.

"I don't know," Jenny replied. If they went anywhere it would be where Lionel went and whenever she tried to talk about it he would say vaguely, "Winter is a long way off and the world is a very large place. We are free to go where we like."

But Jenny had Thomas to think about, however much in love with Lionel she might be. She began to see that she was not quite as free as he was.

Then one autumn morning he packed his belongings and went off to the mainland, saying that he had to finish his university course. He didn't ask Jenny to go with him and by the time she thought of following him she realised he hadn't told her which university he was going to. But he had promised that he would return next summer, after his finals, and he asked her to look after the boat which would be stored for the winter in one of the sheds on the quay. So she was sure that he would come back and that all she had to do was wait. But he didn't write and it was hard to be without him as the winter nights became longer and colder.

Thomas became unhappy too. Silver and her mother had gone away before Lionel, to travel to India, and he asked Jenny several times if they couldn't go there too. But Jenny explained that he wouldn't be able to go to school in India, and it was a long way and they didn't have any money. Thomas couldn't understand why these problems stopped them and not Silver but he knew Jenny was waiting for Lionel and he thought that if Lionel came back then Silver probably would too. And they had the boat. They could go to Happy Island whenever they wanted to.

Because they had lived so cheaply during the summer Jenny had enough money saved from the small allowance Thomas's father still paid into the bank for two months' rent on the caravan. Myra came back too, but not the angry couple. Two of the other caravans were occupied by young teachers who had just taken jobs nearby and were looking for suitable houses to buy, a luxury which seemed unattainable to Jenny. Before Christmas another was taken by Abel Baker's eldest son, Sam, and the girl he had to marry quickly, who forced him to give up fishing and take a job driving a tractor for the District Council. Sam didn't seem to mind his change in circumstances. Chrissie was a pretty girl who grew plump gracefully as the months advanced. She would wait at the caravan door for Sam to come up the path each evening and greet him with a smile and a kiss. Myra was scornful of them but Jenny felt envious. Their happiness bothered her and made her feel even more lonely and she was relieved when Sam and Chrissie moved into a council house before the end of the winter.

Myra said that her book had been quite well received but she had been asked to make some changes before it could be published so she needed more time to work on it. She exclaimed at how brown and healthy Thomas and Jenny looked. She herself was pale and rather fat. She never wore a skirt so Jenny didn't know what her legs looked like but she suspected that Myra's appearance, too, might have been improved by a summer in the sun instead of the city. They told her about their weeks out of doors, which seemed like a dream as they looked out over the grey, stormy waters and wrapped themselves in sweaters and scarves for the daily walk to school.

Jenny enrolled to retake her abandoned Open University course but she needed some money and she didn't like to ask Aunt Patrick for it because she hadn't even sent the old lady a postcard all summer. She looked around for a part-time job but there were a lot of other people in Barly and Innismouth with the same idea and not much work to do until the spring came and it was warm enough to start repainting the hotels and cafés. Joshua Brown looked at Jenny and Myra when he came to collect the rent one Saturday and said, "Pity you two ain't lads. I got my planning permission for the shower blocks up here and you being on the spot could build them easy before the summer."

"We'll do it," Myra said.

"We can't," said Jenny. "We're not strong enough, and besides I don't know how."

"I do," said Myra. "I'll show you. You'll get stronger."

Joshua Brown smiled. The idea was outrageous but it might work and it would give him an excuse to spend time up here talking to the two women. "I'll give you a chance," he said, a gleam in his eye that warned Myra but not Jenny. "You get the foundations laid on time and I'll let you finish the job. I'll come up tomorrow afternoon with the plans."

THREE

The Chairman of the Black Corproation sits in the bar of the Barly and Innismouth Sailing Club, a smartly furnished place with a great deal of polished brass, and colour photographs of large yachts on the walls. He looks speculatively at his son who is in control of their West of England Consortium. Black the Younger is in fact already showing signs of middle age with his short, dark hair greying at the temples and his waistline giving in to the inevitable effects of a lifelong expense account. His tanned face has distinct worry lines on the brow and there's a slight pinkness to his eyeballs. He dresses well. In this quasi-informal atmosphere of a working weekend he's wearing a linen suit and an open-necked shirt. His gold watch and a heavy wedding-ring are the only signs of ornamentation. Black the Elder sees a carbon copy of himself and he is pleased. Apart from a tricky year or two at the settling-down stage his son has conformed well and made a success of his share of the family business.

"How is Elizabeth?" asks Black the Elder, referring to his son's wife.

"She's well. She and the children have gone to stay with her family in Spain. She doesn't like Barly very much. It's a bit too down-market for her taste."

The father nods. "Yes, she does have class. I hope you're not letting her away on her own too much, though. Asking for trouble, that is."

"Elizabeth's all right. She knows the score."

The Sailing Club is situated on a stretch of land at the other side of Barly Beach from the harbour, which the Black Corporation donated to the yachtsmen some years ago on a long lease, and the bar is on the top storey of the clubhouse, with windows on three sides so that it overlooks the estuary, the island, and the harbour. On this spring morning the father and son are sitting at the best table beside the middle window, viewing it all with that satisfaction that can only come from owning as much of it as it has been possible to wrest from the forces of nature.

The Commodore and the Secretary of the Sailing Club, both fairly important people in Innismouth, are sitting at the bar, disgruntled at having their favourite table usurped but knowing better than to be so presumptuous as to join the very important people uninvited. The Blacks are not frequent visitors. They own the Manor House about a mile inland, that once belonged to the Squire Browns, but they only visit for holidays or long weekends from London when they entertain other very important businessmen and their wives. They are, of course, honorary members of the Sailing Club, since they virtually own it, and they like to slip away here for a quiet drink and the opportunity to sound out what they like to think of as local opinion.

"Now tell me," says Black the Elder after they have been served their third round of gin and tonic by the club steward. "What's going on here? Why can't we proceed yet? The Council granted planning permission some weeks ago. The investors are getting impatient."

"It's a little local difficulty. A matter of fishing rights. Down there . . ." He nods towards the harbour. "From time immemorial, or something just as silly, the fishermen have used the quay for their vessels and lived in those cottages. Strictly speaking we can't remove their rights without a special Act of Parliament."

"But we don't want to remove them. We want them to sign them over to us. That's the way we've always operated in the past. It's much cheaper than going to Parliament."

"I understand all that, father, but you know I can't negotiate directly. And the local solicitor we're using is rather jumpy and insisting that things have come to an impasse."

"How bad an impasse? I suppose it's a stubborn group of locals backing each other up?"

"At first, but no longer. They've all sold out except one. That one, in fact." He points a finger down towards the quay where a single small red trawler has just come alongside. On board the trawler the owner is busy fastening warps, then laying out nets. Black the Elder raises a pair of binoculars to his eyes and looks more closely. "My God!" he mutters. "It's a woman!"

"I'm surprised you can tell!" laughs his son.

"And what's the matter with her that she wouldn't rather live in one of our luxury flats instead of a horrible little stone cottage?"

"She's mad."

When they have finished their drinks Black the Elder suggests that they stretch their legs and take a closer look at the cause of the delay that is costing them several thousand pounds a week. They stroll along the quay in the early afternoon sunlight watched by a dozen pairs of eyes that they cannot see. They stand on the edge of the wall looking down on to the deck of the trawler, now several feet below them as the tide drops away. The inevitable smell of stale fish drifts towards them.

"Does she make a living from it?" asks the father.

"I should think so. It's the only real fishing boat left in the place, and there is a demand. The others have all gone over to tourist trips."

"What about a licence? Who issues it?"

"The port authorities up the coast."

"No chance of getting it revoked?"

The son shakes his head. "I've made enquiries. It might

be possible to stop one being issued in the first place, but we haven't got strong enough connections there to put her out of business."

"Pity. Scruffy little boat, isn't it? You wouldn't think it was anyone's pride and joy. I wouldn't be surprised if it sprung a leak quite easily."

"Oh, it seems they're always leaking. Taken for granted. Once it gets too much for the pumps they beach the boat on the sands and mend it."

"It's surprising one doesn't sink every now and again."

"It certainly wouldn't arouse much suspicion."

The next day, before travelling back to London, Black the Elder speaks on the telephone to James Box in his solicitor's office.

"She'll be served with a summons very shortly," James Box is saying. "That'll get her out. Meanwhile we'll have to wait. Be assured by me that it won't be long now." He knows that the Chairman of the Black Corporation is not good at waiting and he's not comfortable about the silence at the other end of the line. He needs Black's business. But he is secure in the knowledge that no other solicitor within a hundred miles will handle it if Black tries to withdraw it from Box and Baffle.

"I see," says Black in what is a well-practised clipped tone. "Well, keep me informed. Pretty poor summer we're having, isn't it? Gales forecast for the Sailing Club cruiser race next week."

"So I understand. But I don't think it'll stop them. Ocean-going cruisers can take pretty well anything."

James Box doesn't think Black is interested in boats, even though he is trying to build a marina, and he is suspicious at the turn in the conversation. He thinks Black has something planned that he isn't being told about and it makes him feel insecure.

★ ★ ★

"I don't know, I must say." Joshua Brown stood over the foundations of his shower block stroking his chin, a mixture of things going through his mind as he eyed Jenny and

Myra up and down. "I didn't think you two could do a proper job but you've proved me wrong."

He'd been so doubtful to begin with that he'd lined up two local builders to take over when the women gave up and now he'd have to tell them they weren't needed after all. He didn't mind that because he was paying Jenny and Myra less than he would have had to pay the men, and having them working for him did nothing to discourage the reputation he had for being "a bit of a lad". They had won him a twenty-pound bet in the pub by finishing the foundations so quickly and expertly and they knew this. They would have done it even more quickly had they not had to retire frequently for cups of tea to avoid the catcalls and unwanted advice from some of the men who seemed to find a walk up to the field an imperative part of their daily routine.

This bothered Jenny more than it did Myra, who was quite good at giving loud wolf whistles herself. Several of the men appeared to find this disconcerting and one or two of them became angry and shouted rudely and didn't come back. Some came every day and just stood and watched silently from a distance. Some walked right up to the work and looked at it, shaking their heads and laughing and saying things like, "That's a strange way to do it. Think it'll last?"

Perhaps they're right, Jenny would think as she went into the caravan to put the kettle on, hoping they would have gone away by the time she came out again. Perhaps we are doing it wrong. But Myra seemed confident. She had helped her father to build a garage once, she said, and there was no mystery about it. "Once you've learned to make things join together you just apply common sense and logic. It's bound to work out right."

It was cold working outside and very tiring. Jenny found herself eating huge meals and falling asleep in front of the television even before Thomas went to bed. Before long she didn't even have the energy to miss Lionel.

Myra was right, they did get stronger. Jenny soon found she could lift surprisingly heavy weights and the muscles in her arms began to swell. She packed away her caftans and wore several thick sweaters bought in jumble sales, with dungarees and wellington boots. Because her long hair tended to get in the way of the cement mixing she plaited it and knotted it at the nape of her neck, then later cut it short. Thomas noticed that when she stroked his face her hands were rough and swollen.

Almost every afternoon Joshua would walk up to the field to see how they were getting on. One day over a cup of tea, when Myra had gone shopping and offered to pick up Thomas from school on her way back, he said to Jenny, "I like you, my dear, I like you a great deal. I wouldn't mind seeing a lot more of you, if you get my meaning."

Jenny did, and she felt shocked and disconcerted. She had always been aware of the way Joshua looked at her, but he looked at Myra that way too, and anyway there were a lot of men around with that particluar gleam in their eyes. It usually went away if she ignored it. She thought of Joshua as being quite old and he was firmly linked in her mind with his lumpy wife Rosie, written off as one of those couples for whom Sex no longer existed. Alone in the evenings she and Myra had laughed about them, and discussed Joshua's reputation, and put it down to bar-room talk with no foundation in fact. Nobody could possibly fancy anyone like him. Now Jenny had to rearrange him in her mind as a sexual predator and she had difficulty with the process.

"I don't think it would be right," she said cautiously to Joshua, unhappily aware that he was her employer and her landlord and she badly needed both the job and the caravan. "I'd much rather keep things the way they are."

He smiled, not at all put out. "You're a nice lass and I respect you for it. But you think on it. I'm a lonely man in some ways and I'd make it worth your while."

Jenny did think on it and it made her feel uncomfortable every time she saw him. But he didn't mention it again and the work progressed satisfactorily so she gradually forgot about it, or at least let it fade into the back of her mind as the winter gradually gave way to early spring.

One warm Sunday in March they took a day off from the building works and made a trip across to Happy Island. They took the boat from the shed on the fishing quay where it was stored for the winter and dragged it down to the beach. Jenny was surprised to find that she and Myra were strong enough to move it between them quite easily. She was sure they could never have managed it a year ago. Determined to show that he was strong too, Thomas heaved the little engine on to his shoulder and followed them. When it was clamped on to the back of the boat and in the water they started it up, not without difficulty, and let it run for a while to make sure it would keep going. Charlie Dog, in his Sunday blazer, ambled out of the Harbour Inn where he was having his lunchtime pint or two, and watched them.

"You ain't going out in that today, are you?"

Jenny looked at him doubtfully, then at the island and the blue water. It all seemed much the same as it had done in the summer and they had come and gone then in what had seemed to her like safety.

"Why not? It was all right in the summer."

"Water's colder now," he said shortly.

"We're not going into the water," Myra said briskly. She never did like being told what to do by anybody, least of all a man.

"Boat's been laid up," Charlie said. "Planks will have dried. She'll take up."

"There's a bailer here," said Thomas. He had learned to bail in the summer. The boat had always leaked a little.

"And that there's a Penguin engine," continued Charlie inexorably. "Well-known for being unreliable, are Penguins."

"It's running all right now," Jenny said doubtfully, "and it ran all the summer."

"Just what I say," Charlie said. "About time it gave out. Unreliable, they are, and they gives out when you least expect it."

"We've got paddles," Thomas said.

Charlie looked out to sea, beyond the bar. "Nasty swell running from the south-west. When the tide's in you'll feel it in the channel. You'll never hold your course with paddles."

"Perhaps we'd better not go," Jenny said. After all, she'd

only been out in the boat before with Lionel or one of the other happies. She'd never been in charge.

"Of course we'll go," said Myra. "It's only a little way and it's a lovely day." And she muttered to Jenny, "You mustn't let these smart-alec locals put you off just because you're a woman."

But Jenny couldn't see that any of Charlie's warnings had anything to do with her being a woman, more with her being inexperienced in boats. She hesitated again, then looked at Thomas's confident, expectant face. He wanted to go over to the island even more than she did. It looked very alluring in the sunlight only a few hundred yards away. "All right," she said, "but we'll only stay a little while."

Charlie shrugged his shoulders and walked back to his pint, though they were sure he was watching them through the windows of the inn as they pushed out the little boat, climbed in, revved up the motor and pointed the bows towards the island. They were across in five minutes with only a little bailing to be done. Every second of those five minutes Jenny was expecting the engine to stop or the bottom boards to open up and she was still shaking when they made a perfect landing on the sands.

"There you are!" said Myra triumphantly. "I told you there was nothing to worry about."

They walked around the island, Jenny saying to Myra, "This is where we had our main camp, this is where we swam, this is where we had the water still," and Myra nodding and saying how wonderful it all looked, and how perhaps she would join them next summer. Jenny thought hopefully of Lionel coming back and Thomas called from the tree house, "It's all just the same up here! Do you think Silver and her mum will come back next summer?" He was excited because he had found it much easier to climb into the tree than before, which showed that he had grown. His one embarrassment with Silver was that she had been taller than him and now he felt that he had a chance to catch her up.

A small cloud scudded across the sun and a brisk gust of wind blew. "Let's get going," said Jenny nervously. If anything went wrong they would be alone and unobserved.

Barly was not a busy place on a Sunday afternoon at this time of year.

Myra deliberately refused to hurry even though Jenny was waiting with water up to the tops of her wellies for quite a few minutes, having difficulty holding the boat off the beach in the swell that was beginning to break against the sands. Thomas jumped in and began bailing right away and as soon as Myra was settled Jenny told her to paddle them off while she started the engine. It choked, then spluttered to life and buzzed them energetically into the middle of the channel where it fluttered and stopped and resisted all Jenny's efforts to restart it. They grabbed the paddles and worked frantically but only succeeded in moving very slowly towards the shore and very fast sideways upstream on the tide into the river estuary.

Finally they grounded a mile from Barly on one of the sand-banks that were just beginning to cover and began to haul the boat along the edge of the sands back to Barly, knee-deep in water. The boat was filling up fast by that time and Thomas was using one of his wellies as well as the bailer to try and keep the water level down. By the time they reached the safety of their own beach the water was up to their waists on the sand-banks and the boat was sinking in spite of Thomas's efforts. Charlie was waiting for them and he helped them to drain the boat and pull it up the slipway on to the quay.

"What went wrong?" he asked casually as they sat halfway up the slipway, resting. "Engine stopped, did it?"

Myra was examining it as Jenny sat shivering and dejected, feeling very foolish.

"Nothing wrong with this engine," Myra declared triumphantly. "It's run out of petrol."

"See," said Charlie. "Told you they was unreliable."

By Easter the shower block was finished to Joshua's satisfaction and Jenny had money in the bank, but the work had curtailed her studies to the point where she hadn't even registered for summer school this year.

"I don't know why you can't get on," Thomas said severely. "I've learned to read and write and I can say my tables up to four-times."

"It isn't the same," Jenny said. "You haven't been building out of doors all day."

Thomas could see that this was true. He would have liked to help more but soon after he arrived home from school each day the work would stop. Once or twice he pretended he wasn't feeling well so that he could be around all day but Jenny made him stay inside to keep warm so that he didn't work. Things improved as the weather warmed up because if the weekends were fine they would work right through and take a rainy day off later in the week. Then he might be given jobs to do like feeding buckets of sand and cement into the mixer, counting them carefully and taking care not to spill the cement powder over himself, or holding pieces of wood in place while they were being sawn up or nailed together.

Thomas recognised that these were very junior jobs but he did his best and was well rewarded the day he was trusted to climb the ladder with a hammer and some nails that Myra had forgotten to take up with her.

Just after Easter Joshua Brown had a dozen new caravans delivered to the field and he told Myra and Jenny that he had let them all from Whitsun.

"Business has never been so good. We're thinking of opening up a shop in the outside kitchen to supply the campers."

"Where will we go?" Thomas asked. "Back to Happy Island?"

Joshua was worrying about that as well. He didn't want them to leave while he thought there was still a chance of persuading Jenny to bed with him and he felt that his chance would increase as soon as Myra had departed for London again. So when he saw the opportunity to keep her nearby and beholden to him he grasped it quickly.

His sister Helen owned a beach café in Innismouth that her father had bought for her when she left school, in order to provide her with employment. Since she had married and gone to Halmouth she had installed a manager in the flat above the café, under the watchful eye of her brother, and she drove over once a week to sign cheques and bank the profits. This situation had been too tempting for the last manager who had diverted a moderate proportion of the profits into his own bank account and had finally been discovered by an astute accountant. Not wanting to appear publicly foolish, Joshua and Helen had decided at the end of the last summer to terminate his employment without taking him to court, so the flat and the manager's job were conveniently vacant just when Joshua was looking for some way to keep Jenny around.

Helen liked the idea of a woman manager, supposing that a woman was more likely to be honest. Jenny accepted the proposition readily, seeing it as a way to independence whilst still being able to look after Thomas. Myra said she was putting herself in an invidious position with regard to Joshua because it was obvious what he was after. Jenny knew without a doubt what he was after, though she wasn't sure what invidious meant. She thought that perhaps Myra was jealous that the job hadn't been offered to her. There didn't seem to be any difficulty in accepting the proposition and making the most of it without compromising herself too far. After all, she had Thomas to think of.

They moved into the flat and she set to work touching up the paintwork and making new table-cloths and curtains.

Some of the happies returned but not Lionel or Silver. One of Lionel's friends sought out Jenny to take possession of the boat and he told her that Lionel had been sent to America by his father to gain experience.

"Experience in what?"

"Business. Lionel's father's a tycoon, you know. Fat cigars and big cars. It's disgusting. Frankly I'm surprised at Lionel giving in. He says it's okay for us to use the boat. Will you be coming across?"

"I have to work." It didn't seem to matter what she did if Lionel wasn't going to be there.

Thomas settled down happily to the new way of life dictated by running the café, finding that it gave him quite a lot of freedom to wander about talking to people, especially the Bakers and the Dogs who would tell him a lot about the weather and the sea and who could sometimes be persuaded to drop him off on the island to see if Silver had come back.

He didn't forget, though, that Jenny mustn't be allowed

to get too tired. When he came home from school in the afternoon he would help her to serve the afternoon teas. At first he was only allowed to carry plates of cakes and dirty dishes back and forth but after a while he became quite good at taking orders and giving change. Visitors thought this was so cute that they came specially to Jenny's café even if they were at the other end of the beach.

Once school broke up he spent quite a lot of time on the island, sleeping there some nights and hitching a lift back and forth in Lionel's boat or with some picnicking family of tourists. Some people muttered at the carelessness of a mother who allowed a small child to wander by himself in such a dangerous situation, but when he heard them Thomas would say that he was nearly eight years old and well able to take care of himself, and his mother too. He always told Jenny where he was going and made sure he was there to help in the café on the busy days of the week.

It was the best summer that Innismouth and Barly had known for the holiday trade. This was due partly to the hot weather which lasted for several unbroken weeks, and partly to the speeding up of the rail service and the improvement of the roads from London and the Midlands. Several families who had never catered for the visitors before opened up their spare rooms for bed-and-breakfast customers and quickly reorganised their domestc lives when they found the demand was steady.

Victor Baker and his younger brother Johnnie gave up using their trawler for fishing, cleaned it up and took parties of plump, pink men on daily rod-and-line trips while their wives spent their time on the beach, keeping an eye on small children made fractious by the heat and too much ice cream. Jimmy Dog painted up an old motor launch that had been sitting in the shed on the quayside for years and ran sightseeing trips up the estaury and along the coast.

"Can't understand them," he was heard to say as he spent his profits over the bar of the Harbour Inn. "Crazy, they must be. Fancy wanting to go to sea for pleasure when they can be safe ashore."

In the autumn the happies went home again and Lionel's friend returned the boat and the motor to Jenny's care, remarking that he had stopped the boat leaking but the motor was becoming more unreliable and needed an overhaul. Jenny took it to the garage in Innismouth who were agents for outboard motors and who were this year displaying a fine new notice saying "Innismouth Marine".

When she asked them if they would service the Penguin they looked at it and laughed. "Throw it away," they said. "It'll cost more to make it work than to buy another."

"But it still goes. It just needs servicing."

"Bloody miracle, then. Won't last much longer."

So she took it home and stood it in a corner of the kitchen and asked Abe and Charlie to help her pull the boat up into the shed.

Joshua's sister was so pleased with the business the café had done that she raised Jenny's wages and postponed her plans to sell the place.

Jenny wore neat, crisp cotton miniskirts, daringly short for Innismouth's tastes, and grew her hair to a shoulder length pageboy with a fringe. Having a job and making a success of it increased her confidence and she became brisk and businesslike and had a cheery smile for everyone. She wrote to Aunt Patrick enclosing a copy of Thomas's latest school photograph and telling her all about the café. Aunt Patrick responded by asking if Jenny had considered yet which prep school to send the boy to, and offering some introductions if there was any difficulty in entering him. She also enclosed a cheque for "little extras" and said she hoped Jenny would soon find something more worthwhile to do with her time. Jenny put the money towards Thomas's first bicycle, a little two-wheeler with detachable balancing wheels at the back, which he soon learned to ride up and down the promenade at high speed. He frightened some old ladies and their dogs as he dodged between them and they complained to Jenny.

"I didn't bump them," he said when she asked him what he had been thinking of. "I didn't even go very close. I'm quite in control, you know."

"I know," Jenny said, "but they don't. You must realise that to them you look just like a rough little boy riding his bike dangerously and if you make them cross they won't come and have their cups of tea in our café any more."

"I see," said Thomas, and he took care after that.

Lifting crates full of lemonade bottles and trays of crockery continued the development of Jenny's muscles that the winter's work had begun. The washing-up did nothing to restore the texture of her hands.

FOUR

"Why didn't you tell me before you did it, you old bugger?" Mrs Baker's voice is hushed and choked for once and tears of rage well in her eyes. She is sitting with old Charlie Dog at her usual corner table in the Harbour Inn. They are both the worse for several pints of extra strong beer, which is nothing unusual.

Charlie sucks on his pipe and watches the flushed face of his friend. "Well, I knowed you be upset and try to stop me, so I thought I'd get it done quick and tell you after."

"I'd have cut off your arms and thrown you in the bloody water," she says. "Here I'm thinking you're one friend I can rely on to stand firm with me and you go and take their money and give up your home and your rights to use the quay. Do you understand what you've done, Charlie?" A large tear splashes into her beer. Charlie has expected anger, not tears, and he doesn't know what to do to put things right. He has never seen her cry.

"I've bought meself some peace and quiet for me old age," he says. "I'm too old to work the boats and I'm too old to fight. The young ones ain't interested, you know that. They make their money with them pleasure launches and their business can only get better. All I want is a place where I can look after myself with all mod cons and sit in the sun and watch the sea. I shall go and live with Jim and his family till the new places are built."

"You'll be there a long while. They can't start till I go and they can't get me out."

"You'll never win, my dear. It'll only cost you money and cause hard feelings. Why don't you give up before any more harm's done?"

"Harm?" She shouts the word as she sits up straight and bangs a fist on the table. "You tell me I'm the one who's causing the harm?" The rest of the bar goes silent for a moment, then continues its conversation with averted eyes, used to this kind of scene from that corner. "Have you no idea what'll happen to this place if they build their monstrosity? Full of snotty yotties and grockles and foreign students? There won't be any real people left."

"You can't stop progress," Charlie says, draining his glass. "Have another drink. What about a short?"

"Thank you very much, Charlie, but I won't if you don't mind. I only accept drinks from my friends." She pours the rest of her beer down her throat in a way that has been the envy of strong men for years and stands up a little unsteadily. As she stomps out of the door the landlord shakes his head and comes over to Charlie to collect the empties.

"You ought to talk to young Thomas," he says. "He's the only one can do something about it now that Abe's gone."

Charlie shakes his head. "He's done his best, poor lad. Can't expect him to be responsible any more. He's got his own way to make." He stares morosely at his glass, wondering whether or not to have a refill. He doesn't enjoy drinking alone. Finally he goes across to the bar and has another pint, sitting on a stool amongst the regulars who have all witnessed the scene with Mrs Baker and take it upon themselves to make what they imagine to be comforting little quips. Charlie pretends that he doesn't care about the quarrel but everyone knows that isn't true.

The following morning, though, when Mrs Baker hammers on Charlie's front door, it's as though their angry parting has never been. They are still old friends and he is the first person she turns to.

Charlie opens the door, already dressed and about to fill his first pipe of the day. "What's up now?" he growls. He always growls early in the morning and she is used to it. She waves a piece of paper at him. "It's arrived! They've sent a summons at last! I had to sign for it, recorded delivery. I'm being summonsed for unlawful use of the quay and unlawful occupation of the land my house is on. Unlawful! I'll soon show them what's lawful! Here, read it!"

Charlie takes the piece of paper and glances at its official court heading, then thrusts it back at her. He can't make any sense of it without his glasses and he forgets where he's put them much of the time. "Looks important, my dear. You'd best pack up then, hadn't you, before they throw you out."

"Pack up be damned! It's out in the open now. I'll fight them all the way and prove in court I've got a right to be here. They won't like what I've got to say in public."

"Watch out for them solicitors," Charlie says, wagging his pipe stem at her. "They'll twist you up in knots unless you got one in your own pay, and that'll cost you a packet, you mark my words."

"Justice shouldn't cost money. I know my rights and I'll tell them. I don't need a solicitor to put pieces of paper in front of a judge."

James Box wants to be remembered as the chairman of the council that put Innismouth on the big-time tourist map. Next spring he'll be fighting an election again, though in Innismouth it's not so much a fight as a gentle amble, and a successful development plan will make a better impression than a public scandal. He really wants the Black Corporation to be named as plaintiffs in the court case against Mrs Baker but Black the Younger has pointed out that the quay and the cottages and the Harbour Inn and the shop are all part of a compulsory purchase package, so it's really the Council which must take steps to remove her.

They have come close to having a dispute about this as they sit in James Box's office, the most imposing in the suite that Box and Baffle own in a large Victorian mansion overlooking the sea at the furthest end of Innismouth from Barly. James Box is rather proud of the tasteful mahogany panelling, the leather upholstery and the deep pile carpet. Black compares it unfavourably with the elegant and expensive office suite in the City of London that his father wants him temporarily to abandon, and thinks how predictable and unimaginative provincial taste is.

"What about costs?" asks Box.

"You'll be awarded costs against her. You know that."

"But she may not have the capital to pay. They say she gave it all to her son years ago."

"She still owns her trawler. They can impound that to recover the costs."

"What if she wins? The damages might be enormous."

"How can she win?" It's this doubting attitude, which many might construe as caution in the public interest, that makes Black impatient with men like Box. His father has shown him that it is easier and cheaper in the long run to work amicably with public officers, however parochial their outlook may be. But this one is proving exceptionally difficult. There are other firms of solicitors who can be brought in. Changes will have to be made if this prevarication goes on.

"We have to be careful," Box insists, angry that he feels any anxiety at all, let alone that he is having difficulty in hiding that anxiety from Black. "Public money is at stake."

"And every day's delay is costing our investors even more money," says Black, not for the first time. "We can't wait much longer."

"You may not have any choice."

"There is always a choice."

For the first time it occurs to James Box that if he works in the public interest he may lose the support of the Black Corporation, and if he gives the Corporation precedence he may be in difficulty with his electorate. And all because of a drunken woman and a trawler.

★ ★ ★

In the spring Jenny received a letter from Aunt Patrick, written in a more spidery scrawl than usual. The old lady had fallen while stepping out of a lift in Harrods and had broken her leg. She was in a nursing home in Knightsbridge and she would welcome a visit from her only living relatives. She sent a cheque for their train fares and a generous additional sum for new clothes for Thomas because she knew how children grew.

When she was reading the letter, sitting at the breakfast table, Jenny glanced across at Thomas who was sprawled on the floor reading a book about sailing ships. What sort of impression would he make on her aunt, she wondered? He certainly had grown. If it had been a weekday he would have been wearing some semblance of a school uniform which always looked neutrally scruffy. But today was Saturday and he was dressed in old jeans wearing very thin on the seat, a jersey that Mrs Sing had passed on to them which was too small for him and was coming unravelled at one wrist, and gym shoes tied with string instead of laces. His reddish hair was really too long, even by the current fashion.

"Thomas," she said, "are those the only jeans you've got?"

"No," he replied, without looking up, "but all the others are too small."

"And what about that sweater I bought you after Christmas?"

"Too scratchy round the neck."

"And your shoes? You had a new pair of sandals last week."

This time he did look up and his eyes were evasive. "Forgotten," he said briefly.

"What do you mean, forgotten?"

"Well, yesterday I was walking back from school along the beach and the tide was a bit too far in so I had to paddle to get round the rocks. I took off my sandals and socks so as not to get them wet. Then a bit further on I put them down to have a good look at some string I'd found and I forgot them."

"Oh Thomas! That's the third pair in a year!"

"I'm sorry, Mum, really I am. I went back later but the

tide had already got them." Then he added cheerfully, "It can't be unusual, you know. I find a lot of shoes washed up on the beach, though they're never mine. What's the matter anyway? You never usually complain about the way I look."

"We're going to London to visit Aunt Patrick. I want you to be smart."

When she had heard Jenny's account of the café and Thomas's progress at school Aunt Patrick said, "You should settle down and do something with your life. Running a beach café and sending him to the local government school may be all right as a short-term measure but it won't get you anywhere in the long run, you know."

She looked very frail and thin lying there in the high bed, her silver hair carefully set in gentle waves and covered with a gossamer net. She wore a pink crochet bed-jacket and her silver-capped walking stick was lying alongside her on the bedcover, as though she might grasp it and leap up for a walkabout at any moment though the nurse had told them that she hadn't been out of bed for a month and was unlikely to for some time to come. Her leg was healing only very slowly, as was often the case with old people, and it was nice that she had some visitors from her family at last.

"Where do you think I should be going?" Earning her own living and taking care of Thomas seemed enough for the time being.

"You must mix with the right type of people. You owe it to Thomas to find him a father."

"I've got a father, haven't I?" asked Thomas. "We just don't see him. Mum says she doesn't like him very much."

Aunt Patrick ignored him, as she always did children. "You must come back to London and find yourself a proper job; be a personal assistant or something. You're quite good at organising things. Take up tennis and join a social club. I'll arrange some introductions for you. And send that boy to a proper school where he won't be allowed to look like a gypsy most of the time."

"I can't afford that," Jenny said with relief.

"Yes you can. I've made my will in your favour. When I die they'll sell my flat in Pont Street and after the bill here is paid all the proceeds are for you and Thomas, with the one proviso that you don't have any of it unless it's to be spent on something worthwhile."

"Who's to say what's worthwhile?"

"My solicitor. I've briefed him thoroughly. There's to be no frittering of cash on nonsense, you understand. With money behind you there should be no problem finding a husband. But you really must stop doing all this menial work and take more care of your hands."

Travelling back on the train Jenny pondered on Aunt Patrick's view of the best way to find herself security. Poor Aunt Patrick, it wasn't her fault. It was the system she'd been brought up to understand. Life was different now.

Thomas had shrugged off his new jacket and loosened his tie and was sprawled on the seat opposite her, reading a paperback he had bought at Paddington Station about a boy who'd stowed away on a sailing ship. His new corduroy trousers were already grubby at the knees and his new lace-up shoes had scuff marks on the toes. He looked up at Jenny and grinned. "Nice to be going home, isn't it, Mum?"

Jenny smiled. How could she ever even think of sending him away to school? Their home was together; Barly and Innismouth, the sea, the café. Then she remembered Joshua and her smile became cynical. She wanted to dismiss Aunt Patrick as having an outlook that was out of date, but where was the difference really between Aunt Patrick's world and hers?

Joshua had never actually said that if she didn't sleep with him she would lose the café but since she had given in to his repeated requests to see more of her (and he had seen just about all of her now) she had felt a lot more secure. She did have pangs of guilt, not because of Rosie whom she didn't meet very often now, but because she couldn't seem to get around to feeling any love for Joshua however much he said he cared for her and tried to prove it.

Even though she had finally admitted to herself that Lionel had well and truly exercised his right to be free, she still felt a lingering yearning for him and Joshua wasn't really the person to take his place. He liked to call on her unobserved on dark winter evenings after Thomas was asleep, combining his visits with a drink at one of the pubs to give himself an alibi. Although he was cheerful company and brought her little presents from time to time, he never had to stay long to fulfil his needs, which rarely gave her time to achieve an orgasm. After an hour he would set off back to his comfortable home and his wife. This annoyed Jenny at first but after a while she began to see the value of having a lover who didn't intrude into any more of her life than was necessary. She had time to get on with her housework and get her accounts for the business up to date, a task she found impossible during the busy summer season. To the rest of Innismouth and Barly she was free and independent and Joshua was never, never anything other than distant and businesslike when Thomas was around.

One day Thomas looked up from his tea and said, "We've started doing a project on engines at school. They're ever so simple. Only three things can go wrong with them, you know: no fuel, no air, or no spark."

"If they're that simple why does everyone make such a fuss about them?" Jenny said, barely looking up from her book. By way of pleasing Aunt Patrick she had started her Open University Foundation Course again, hoping that a degree would qualify her for the kind of job the old lady seemed to think she should be doing.

"People only make a fuss when they don't know. Look." Thomas took out his exercise book and showed her some fairly competent drawings of pistons, cylinders, spark plugs and carburettors, and he patiently explained to her what they all did. She set aside her own work and tried to concentrate on what he was telling her because she had recently read how important it was to encourage children by giving them attention. They took the exercise book over to the Penguin outboard, which still sat in the corner of the kitchen gathering dust, and tried to find the parts that corresponded to Thomas's drawings. It wasn't so simple after all but Thomas said they had a small engine at school they were taking to pieces and he promised to find out more and come back and tell her. "Perhaps you could get some useful books from the library," he suggested.

During the next few weeks the little engine gradually spread to take up more and more space in the flat. Pieces were removed and carefully numbered and entered on a diagram pinned to the living-room wall. Jenny spent money on spanners and on new parts to replace those that seemed bent or worn. Then for a while the reassembled engine was clamped to the back of the kitchen chair with its propeller in a plastic waste bin half full of water and tested every evening. This could be interesting because once the propeller was revolving the water was unlikely to remain in the bin and if Thomas took too long making any necessary adjustments there could be quite a flood. Jenny didn't mind mopping up the floor but the damp stain on the ceiling of the café kitchen gave her cause for worry. She was afraid Helen might not be understanding if she asked for it to be redecorated yet again, and she thought that if it got very wet the plaster might collapse altogether.

In the end the engine worked satisfactorily every time they started it and Thomas and Jenny felt very pleased with themselves. They decided to try it out on the boat as soon as the weather improved and spring showed signs of being on the way.

The time spent on the engine caused Jenny to be late with two assignments in a row and she wondered anxiously if it wouldn't be better for Thomas if she concentrated on the long-term future instead of spending her time helping him to put engines together.

Jenny needn't have worried about the kitchen ceiling because when she saw the annual accounts, Joshua's sister was so pleased with the previous year's business that she paid for a complete redecoration and bought a new counter with a showcase for the scones and cakes to be more hygienically displayed. While Jenny was busy hanging curtains Thomas said, "I could put up some shelves and have little ornaments and things for sale."

"That won't be any good. They sell souvenirs in the newsagents down the road. We'd be in competition with them and then neither of us would do well. We wouldn't like it if they started to sell cups of tea."

"We must think of something different then. Suppose I try making some model boats?"

"All right," Jenny said indulgently. At least the trying

would keep him busy for a while. Since the refurbishment of the café had begun she hadn't had time to give Thomas the attention he needed and she was worried about the effect this might be having on his development. It would be terrible if Aunt Patrick turned out to be right and he had to go to boarding school. She promised herself that next year she would have more time and they would go for long walks together and even take a short holiday abroad. Travel would be good for him.

At Whitsun, just when they were ready to reopen for the season, Jenny was alarmed but not surprised to find herself pregnant. Ever since her liaison with Joshua had begun she had found it difficult to come to grips with the problem of contraceptives. She could have asked her doctor, a stiff, elderly lady, but she knew from what she had heard about other people that private medical details were not sacred to the officious secretary who worked at the reception desk. There was a clinic in Halmouth but getting there took a bit of organising and meant a long bus journey. She had known she must make the effort soon, and made vague plans, while Joshua complained about having to use "them silly rubber things" and frequently got impatient, taking them off without her knowledge so that he could get into her more easily.

So she had to go to the doctor after all and admit that she had a sex life and the doctor clucked her tongue and asked for a sample of urine, and then asked what Jenny thought she wanted to do about it.

"What do you mean, do about it? I suppose I could have it adopted . . ."

"Er . . . no need to have it at all." The doctor peered over the top of her glasses. "Single mother, no visible means of support, sexually promiscuous, mentally unstable—no difficulty in getting you an abortion as far as I can see."

Jenny flushed. "I'm not all those things. I earn my own living and I don't sleep around."

The doctor gave her a look that indicated total disbelief and said, "Everyone knows about Joshua Brown and his little fancies, my dear. This isn't the first time, you know. I'll give you a letter for the specialist in Halmouth. Wait outside while my receptionist makes an appointment."

She had to sit under the scornful gaze of the receptionist while telephone calls were made, and travel to Halmouth the following week. She wished she'd taken the trouble earlier. The specialist was old and bald and had fat, scaly hands. Jenny wondered why it always seemed to be men who acquired an intimate professional knowledge of women's insides. He gave her a painful internal examination that she was sure was more detailed than necessary, but she was in no position either physically or morally to complain with any dignity.

He looked at her with little watery eyes through thick, rimless spectacles and said, "Next week, two days in hospital and it'll all be over." She decided at that moment that rather than have this man anywhere near her insides again she would have Joshua's baby and somehow manage to look after it, as she had managed with Thomas. Thomas might even like to have a little sister or brother.

That evening she told Joshua what had happened and what she was going to do. He looked concerned and held her hand and said, "Don't worry, I'll see you're all right. But you'll have to go away from here, somewhere where nobody knows you. Perhaps you could go back to London."

"I don't want to go away. We like it here, Thomas and I."

"That's no odds to me, my dear." His eyes lost their laughter and became hard. "You've got yourself into trouble and I can't be doing with that on my doorstep."

The following week Jenny received a letter from Helen saying that she was planning to sell the café after all and giving her a month's notice to quit the job and the flat. As she read it she couldn't control her feelings.

"Why are you crying, Mum?" asked Thomas, looking up from the model boat he was making. By that time he was quite proficient at this, working from drawings in books and whittling away at old pieces of driftwood with a knife that Jenny thought was rather too sharp but hadn't the heart to take away from him.

"Mr Brown's sister wants to sell the café. We'll have to go."

Thomas's lips clenched in a hard line as he turned back to

his work. Without looking round again he said, "It would be nice if we could buy the café wouldn't it? Then no one could make us go."

"We haven't any money."

After a pause Thomas said, "Silver told me that Lionel was quite rich really. Perhaps he'll come back and buy it for us."

"Perhaps."

"If I was rich I'd buy it." There was a silence while they both contemplated these impossible dreams, then Thomas said, "We can always go back to the island."

"Yes." They'd lived there once, they could do so again.

"Can we go and have a look at it tomorrow?"

"The boat's rotten. I looked at it this morning." She had asked Victor Baker to take it down to the water thinking, like Thomas, that it would be nice to look at Happy Island. But they could see daylight between two of the bottom boards and Vic had said, "It needs work."

"We can do it," Thomas said. "We can mend things and paint. Let's go and have a look and see what needs doing."

With help and advice from Vic and his father, and anyone else who was passing and had time to stop and talk, the repairs to the boat took only a few days. Jenny almost forgot her troubles as they replaced the rotten planks, then stripped off the old paint and varnish and gave it what Thomas called "a new suit of clothes". When the happies came back this year they would hardly recognise it.

That same week Aunt Patrick fell victim to an influenza epidemic. Jenny travelled up to the funeral leaving Thomas in the care of Sarah Baker. There were not many people at the graveside, just a few old ladies and one old gentleman who wore a pink rose in the lapel of a very worn alpaca coat and blew his nose heavily on several occasions. They seemed to know who Jenny was even though she didn't know them and they all shook her hand gravely before driving away in large cars. Jenny made her way to a solicitor's office in Holborn and sat in a large leather armchair while a very handsome and prosperous looking young man, with blond hair and a fine suntan above his city suit, read out Aunt Patrick's will, which was short and uncomplicated as to its business but contained a lengthy sermon as to the virtues of settling down.

"Do you think," asked Jenny when he had finished, "that buying a thriving business and running it would constitute 'settling down'?"

"It might. What have you in mind?"

"A tourist café in the place where I live. I believe it's on the market."

"I could look into it."

"I'd like you to. Right away. And I don't want the vendors to know you're acting for me. They don't approve of women in business, you see."

He smiled warmly. "I didn't know your aunt for long, Mrs Sharpe, only since I took over her affairs from my uncle when he retired recently. But I can see that you take after her. I'd be pleased to act for you in any way you require. Shall we discuss the details over dinner?"

A month later Jenny owned the café and she put up a big notice saying "Under New Management" and changed the name to *Jenny's*. While she was repainting the sign she slipped and fell off the ladder and miscarried the baby.

She had to spend a few days in hospital and they warned her that she would feel very tired and depressed for a while after she went home. She waited nervously for this depression to overcome her but as each day passed she felt fitter and more cheerful than ever before in her life. At last she had the financial means to look after Thomas properly and this gave her a great sense of security.

Whenever she passed Joshua in the street, if he hadn't seen her first and managed to cross out of her way, she would smile brightly and say, "Good morning, Joshua! Lovely day!" He would mumble something and avert his eyes, then glance back towards her waistline. The anxious, questioning look on his face gave her great pleasure.

During that summer she put on a little weight for the first time. Feeling that she needed to keep up her strength after the miscarriage she nibbled a lot between meals, then she decided it wasn't wise to diet while she was so busy. She would concentrate on getting her figure back in trim later in the year.

Because running her own business took even more of her time and attention than managing someone else's, she gave up trying to do her Open University course and she never bothered to enrol again.

FIVE

"THE INNIS ESTUARY—A HAVEN OF PEACE FOR HOLIDAY-MAKERS" ran the headline in the holiday supplement of a national newspaper shortly after Christmas.

"One of the unspoiled parts of the West Country coastline, that is now more readily accessible to holidaymakers from the city with the completion of the M4–M5 link, is the Innis Estuary, with the quiet and dignified town of Innismouth and the harbour village of Barly still offering the kind of attractions that brought Victorian families flocking there when the Great Western Railway was first opened. Whether your idea of holiday pleasure is to lie on a fine sandy beach, walk the cliffs or the sands, watch the wide variety of rare wild birds, fish, or trail your own boat down to the safe waters of the estuary, this is the place for you. Set in outstandingly beautiful countryside, the estuary offers a few quality hotels and guesthouses, one or two good restaurants, and a discreet campsite for those with more limited pockets."

"Well," said Mrs Sing as she passed the paper across the counter to Jenny. "That'll finish our peace and quiet, for sure."

THE LIFE AND TIMES OF BARLY BEACH

The Council Amenities Committee decided to build a row of beach huts at one end of the promenade and buy a thousand new deckchairs.

Joshua Brown filled another field with caravans and applied for planning permission to convert his cowsheds into a clubhouse and bar for his campers.

★ ★ ★

Rufus Black has finally persuaded his son of the wisdom of moving semi-permanently into the Manor House at Barly whilst the new development is under way. It will enable close supervision of the project and also will create a good impression with the public, many of whom may be quite put out when they realise the full extent of what is being done. The fact that the younger Black and his family are content to live nearby themselves will to some extent alleviate any criticism. The fact that they will move as soon as the changes have been made is irrelevant.

"Elizabeth won't be at all happy," says the younger Black as they discuss arrangements in the Black Corporation's London headquarters, high above the City traffic. "You know how she dislikes Barly."

"I can't see the problem. A couple of years living by the seaside, out of the rat race. It'll be so good for the children. And there's the fast rail-link to London from Halmouth."

"She just hates small towns."

"Increase her allowance. And make sure she joins things—helps to raise money and all that sort of thing. It creates a good impression. Now, about this boat. What have you decided on?"

"I've decided to draw the line. No boat. I hate anything to do with boats. It's bad enough having to be buried by the seaside. No boat."

"You must have a boat. You're a leading member of the local Sailing Club and we're involved in turning the River Innis into one of the major yachting centres in the West. You must have a boat. You don't have to take it anywhere. Just put it on a mooring and use it to impress people. I've been looking around. There's an almost brand new fifty-foot Easterly *Warrior* up for sale at Cowes. Fitted out for some Arabian prince who's since been assassinated. We'll go and have a look at it tomorrow."

"An Easterly? You mean it has a mast? And sails?"

Black the Elder is disappointed and impatient with his son for the first time in many years. He has never seen him turn pale before and he even notices a slight tremble of the hand as he lights his cigar.

"It also has a very large engine. What is the matter with you? I'm not asking you to sail it. I'm not even asking you to pay for it."

In due course the yacht is brought round from Cowes to the Innis Estuary and the Sailing Club Committee are only too pleased to allocate a prime mooring to such an impressive vessel belonging to one of their most important members. It rides on the water in full view of the windows of the bar, admired by all. Many hints are dropped by members willing to act as crew on one of her shakedown cruises. Mr Black intimates that this will be soon but that he is pressurised by business commitments at present. Meanwhile he entertains his associates on board, reaching the mooring by means of a smart launch with two large new Japanese outboard motors. He explains to them that when the marina, in which they have invested their money, has been built, there will be no need for the inconvenience of the launch trip which can sometimes be a little wet. They will be able to step straight on board from a pontoon.

He talks vaguely of plans for a trip to the Channel Islands, because he has heard that this is where yachtsmen go for a weekend cruise, but he doesn't admit that he has no idea how to find them, or how to hoist the sails. He is looking around for someone he can trust enough to help him overcome these shortcomings.

The only yacht in the estuary which in any way rivals the Easterly, either in size or sleekness of line, is the one that Thomas Sharpe has built to enter the Baltic Race. It annoys Black when his visitors comment on it but it can't be ignored, swinging gracefully on its mooring half a mile up river from the club, near the channel that leads to Sharpe's boat yard at Innstone. He listens carefully to what they say in the club bar about its possible shortcomings: too narrow in the beam, too shallow a draught, too simple a rig, wood construction is out of date. It'll never go well in light winds, in strong winds, in a heavy sea. He repeats these comments to his visitors and they nod in admiration of his knowledge and ask if he'll be entering his yacht for any of the big races. Black replies that he's thinking about it, but of course it's difficult finding the time.

Rodney Pritchard, retired naval officer and present Commodore of the club, assures him that the Easterly will more than hold its own in any race. Now that Black spends more time in Barly, Commodore Pritchard is quite relaxed about chatting to him in the bar and even waving to him on the mooring if he passes in his own small cruiser.

"Have to make a few modifications, of course, old boy, but nothing complicated or expensive. More sails, really, and some extra winches and stronger rigging."

Black nods. "It just isn't worth it. With my commitments I haven't time to attend to it and then I can't take time away to try her out. Even if everything goes according to plan I might be called away at the last moment. I'm not like you retired people, living a quiet life by the sea!"

"What you need," says Pritchard carefully, "is a professional skipper to do all the nitty-gritty. Then you just sail as owner and take all the credit."

"And sign the cheques, no doubt!"

But Black begins to like the idea of a professional skipper. Sailing like that he can pick up a bit of expertise without appearing to be too ignorant. Next time he meets Commodore Pritchard he asks him where a man of the necessary calibre can be found.

"Right here," replies the Commodore. "I used to race with Jed Field."

The legendary name of Jed Field causes a hush in most yachting circles but Black the Younger has never heard of him. He assumes, though, that this is impressive or it wouldn't have been mentioned, so he raises his eyebrows and says, "Really?"

"Yes, indeed. I'll do the job for you, and find you a good crew. You leave it to me, old boy."

★ ★ ★

For much of Jenny and Thomas's fourth summer in Innismouth the weather was poor and though it didn't keep the tourists away it put an end to the happy camp. Three of them came and borrowed the boat and spent a few disconsolate days in wet tents, then they departed for warmer shores and never came back. Thomas asked after Silver and her mother but nobody seemed to know whether they had ever returned from India.

Finding himself more or less in sole possession of the boat, Thomas put up a little notice on Barly Quay and took people out for trips to the island or up the estuary when he was free after school or at the weekends. His customers were always alarmed at first to find such a small boatman in charge but when they saw that he seemed to know what he was doing, and they arrived back safely, they decided that managing a boat must be easier than it looked. If he liked the people and they listened to what he told them about the tides, he would hire them the boat for the whole day while he was at school.

That summer the Council had decided that it should control and register all the pleasure launches, for purposes of safety and also because the licence fee brought them extra revenue. Although Thomas would have been very willing to apply for a licence if anyone had told him he needed one, he never did because no official who read his notice believed that he was doing anything other than playing games.

Jenny was busy running the café and supervising the two waitresses she had taken on to deal with the increased business and she didn't know about Thomas's boating enterprises for some time. When she found out it seemed too late to try to stop him. As he pointed out, he had never had an accident and he had a nice sum of money in his Post Office account. She did buy him a life-jacket but he realised that it wouldn't give his customers much confidence so he only wore it if he took Jenny out for a picnic on one of her rare days off.

The number of craft in the estuary was increasing. So far there had been the trawlers, followed by the pleasure launches and a few small day sailing boats, mostly varnished wood owned by people who lived in houses along the river.

They would set forth on the finer days for little trips around the place. One or two crusing yachts would nose into the estuary occasionally and drop anchor up river of the harbour but it had never been a popular place with them because of the bar and the island which made the entrance treacherous to all but those who knew their way well. But since the article in the national paper more and more people brought sailing boats down to the coast on trailers behind their cars, and they would leave them parked on Barly Beach above the tide-line for the duration of their holidays and take them away again.

Some visitors became more permanent. The houses in and around Innismouth and Barly were still cheap then and attracted a growing number of retired people, many of whom wanted to keep boats. In the parts of the estuary that were protected from the tidal currents they laid concrete moorings with large floating buoys at the end of their chains. These were much safer for the boats than anchoring them but not much appreciated by Charlie and Abe and their families who found it hazardous enough taking their trawlers and launches in and out of the estuary without the added problems of becoming hooked up on a newly laid mooring. If a mooring line became entangled in their rudders or propellers their consolation was in cutting the buoy adrift in order to free themselves, which caused bad feeling. But they would shrug and say, "We were here first. Our boats is our living. Who ever heard of putting out to sea for fun when you don't have to. Crazy lot, yotties."

However, crazy or not, the yotties appeared to be happy, except when their moorings had been fouled by the pleasure launches or fishing boats. On Saturdays and Sundays they would putter out to their yachts in small dinghies with little outboard motors that sometimes worked but very often didn't, to judge by the number of them who could be seen rowing energetically with an outboard fixed to the back of the boat. They would paint and clean, and sit in their cockpits eating and drinking in the sun. Sometimes they would even spend a night aboard and occasionally, if the tide and the weather were just right, they would put out to sea for a day or so and return flushed with triumph to swap stories in the Harbour Inn about how well they had done.

Sometimes on the moorings there would be a touch of excitement as somebody fell in the water, or skippers had high-pitched arguments with their crews, forgetting how sound travels across water. Abe and Charlie and their boys would sit on the quay smoking or mending nets and waiting for the tide and smile to each other. In the winter the yotties would put their boats away in boatyards and front gardens and go to navigation classes at night school, where they learnt all about buoyage and plotting courses and the Rules of the Road, so that they could return to the water the following year and tack their yachts along the main channel and shout furiously to Victor or Charlie, or whoever might be trying to motor up the channel in the opposite direction, "Rule eighteen! Rule eighteen! Get out of the way, you bloody fool!"

"What's this rule eighteen, then?" Vic asked Charlie one evening when he had narrowly avoided a collision with an erratically steered yacht and grounded on a sand-bank as a result.

Charlie scratched his head. "I think it's the one that says if you got a motor you got to keep out of the way of sailing vessels."

Vic looked perplexed. "You mean they was in the right, running me aground?"

Charlie shook his head. "No. There's another rule which says if you're in a narrow channel, or going about your business in a proper manner, they got to avoid you. But perhaps they haven't got to that bit yet in their classes."

Another memorable feature of that summer was Lionel's reappearance in Jenny's life. In some respects it was just as she had imagined it might be in her more rose-tinted dreams, but overall it was a major disaster.

It was late in the summer, at a quiet period of the day, just as lunches had finished and teas not yet begun Jenny and her waitresses had a rota for this time and Jenny was just about to go off duty for a couple of hours when she noticed a tall, dark-haired young man in a business suit peering in through the window. People often did this before they decided to come in so she thought nothing of it and when he finally did push open the door she called out, "We are open, but only for snacks. Lunches are finished, I'm afraid."

He hesitated and blinked and said, "I don't want lunch. I think it's you I want. You are Jenny, aren't you?"

"Yes, that's right, but who . . . ?"

Wearing those clothes he was certainly not a holiday visitor. Now that she could see him better she noticed that his suit and shoes were well-made and expensive, so he couldn't be a salesman—not of anything she could afford to buy, anyway. His face was fine-boned and thin and his suntan had the golden glow of more concentrated and careful treatment than England could have afforded it that summer. He was the sort of young man to whom Aunt Patrick would have given her approval and as there was something vaguely familiar about his smile she wondered if he was from the solicitor's office in London. He carried a pigskin briefcase on which were embossed in gold leaf the initials L.B.

His smile spread and took on a rather foolish aspect as his eyes betrayed his disappointment that she didn't know who he was. "You must remember me. I know I've changed, but so have you. It's Lionel."

"Oh!" It was her turn to feel foolish. But without the beard and the large toes sticking out of his sandals it was very difficult. Even now that he had told her she couldn't really be sure. She had to take his word for it. Then she had to wonder whether she was really pleased to see him or not. After all, he had gone off two years ago and made no attempt to contact her. "Would you like a cup of tea?" she asked, realising how inadequate it sounded as a greeting to a long-lost lover.

"Not really. What I'd like is a trip to the island. Have you still got the boat?"

"Oh yes." Thomas had started the new school term this week and she hoped he hadn't hired it out for the day. "It's probably down at Barly. We'll go across and see."

As they walked together the half-mile across the point that separated Innismouth from Barly he commented, "This place seems far busier than it was."

"Lots more people are coming here," she said but she was so preoccupied with memories of how it used to be between them and the way it might come to be again that she hardly heard the "Mmmm . . ." he gave in reply and completely missed the speculative note in his voice.

The boat was pulled up on the beach above the high water mark and Lionel commented approvingly on how smart and well-kept it looked. Jenny glowed with pride. He put his briefcase in the bows and helped her push it down the beach on the little trolley Thomas had built for it. He stood back as it slid into the water to avoid getting his footwear wet. Jenny threw her sandals into the boat and stood up to her knees in water so that he could jump in and still keep dry. She laughed and commented that his present disguise didn't suit him much.

"It's important to conform in business circles," he said.

"What business are you in?"

"I work for my father. Property development."

She had sort of expected him to take charge of the boat but he placed himself amidships, so she paddled off the shore and started the engine and steered them across the water, heading upstream to allow for the outgoing tide.

It was a bright and sparkling day, one of the few so far that summer, and two families had drawn up their boats on the island for picnics, and to explore. Jenny walked beside Lionel as she had done in the past, stopping when he stopped to gaze around, mentally noting all the old haunts, as she always did when she came across.

He said little and she stood quite close to him, hoping that he would turn to kiss her when he had absorbed enough of the atmosphere. Finally they came to a spot amongst the trees, looking across to the far side of the estuary, which had been one of their favourite places for making love. He laid down his briefcase and sat down and she sat beside him, remembering. Then he turned to her and said, "How big do you think this place is?"

"How big?" She struggled to understand what he was talking about.

"Yes. How many acres, or square miles?"

"Goodness only knows. Why does it matter? Are you thinking of declaring yourself king?"

He looked at her distantly, almost with distaste. "Don't be silly. You haven't grown up at all, have you?"

"Was there any need to?"

"I thought you might have become less irresponsible by now. I know I have."

She began to realise that the prosperous businessman image might not be a disguise. This might be the real Lionel—the only Lionel.

"In that case, why have you come back here today?"

"To do a job for my father. To assess our assets in Barly."

"Assets?"

"Yes. Land. For development."

"But assets are what you already own."

"That's right. My father bought the Manor House years ago—for us to come down to for holidays. He saw the potential of a spot like this and he's been buying up pieces of property ever since."

"I thought some relatives of the Browns owned the Manor . . . Oh, I suppose you're them."

"That's right. My father and Joshua's wife are cousins. That's why he came here in the first place. Between them they own most of the undeveloped land for a mile or two along this estuary. Except for the harbour. The Council owns that."

"I'm very glad to hear it. I suppose you own the island then?"

"That's right. And the beach."

"I thought it was all public land."

"Most people do. It doesn't matter for the time being. We don't want to develop it yet. The value isn't right."

"Value?"

"The place isn't sufficiently popular yet. Not enough people living here. But that'll come."

Jenny couldn't see the view properly any more. She began to feel cold, and not only because the skies were clouding over. "Lucky for you that article went into the paper to set things on their way." Then she realised, even before he spoke.

"No luck about it. These things have to be carefully organised." He stood up. "Well, shall we be getting on our way? I think I've seen all I want to see. And just for old times' sake, take a tip from me. If you can buy up any cheap bits of property hereabouts, get hold of them and hang on to them. I shouldn't really tell you that, of course, but there's no harm in you being able to make a little killing for yourself. How's young Thomas?"

It began to rain as they walked back to the other side of the island, first a few drops then a gentle drizzle that made Lionel's well-groomed hair fall forwards over his eyes and his expensive suit hang limply from his shoulders. The picnicking families began to pack up and push their boats on to the water.

Half-way across the channel Lionel commented on how well the outboard motor was running and no sooner had he spoken than it choked and cut out. "Fool!" exclaimed Jenny crossly.

"It's only an engine. You can't call it a fool because it won't go."

"I meant you! You used to drive this engine. You must have learned that any outboard motor automatically stops if you say it's going well."

"Do stop being silly, Jenny, and just get it started again."

"I may not be able to." She leaned over the stern of the boat. "There's something jamming the prop. Probably a bit of fishing line. It'll take ages to get it off. You'd better start paddling." They had already been swept several hundred yards out of the estuary mouth. The harbour wall slipped from sight behind the point and Innismouth beach began to slide past them, deserted because of the rain which now fell steadily. Lionel took up a paddle from the bottom of the boat and began to dip it gently in and out of the water, which made no difference at all to their progress.

"Harder," snapped Jenny, still leaning over the engine.

"Why don't you help? There's another paddle."

"I've got to get this thing inboard and free it."

"You haven't time. We're being swept out to sea." There was a slight hint of panic in his voice.

"Paddle us towards the beach. Hard." She had freed the

bolt holding the engine in place and leaned over even further to lift it aboard. Lionel shifted his position sideways to get a better purchase on the water. The boat lurched violently and the engine jumped out of Jenny's hands. It fell with a triumphant plop into the water and sank immediately. She remembered that Thomas had told her always to tie it on with a piece of cord as well as bolting it but of course she had forgotten about that today with the excitement of seeing Lionel again.

In order to grip the boat with both hands Lionel let go of the paddle. "Oh my God!" he exclaimed as he watched it float away. Then he turned towards the beach and shouted "Help!" several times.

"It's no good. No one can hear you from here. You must stand up and raise and lower your arms."

"Stand up in this tub? We"ll go overboard next."

Calmly Jenny did as she had advocated but there was no response from the deserted beach. She took up the second paddle and tried to make way against the tide but they had gone too far.

Out of the shelter of the estuary the sea was choppy and several small waves broke over the bows into the boat, wetting Lionel's smart briefcase. He moved it around a few times, hoping to keep it dry, before he realised they had more important things to worry about. The boat felt very small and unstable on the open seas. They were soon soaked and very cold. After turning pale with fright beneath his suntan Lionel began to look a blotchy green and shivered violently.

"Will we be rescued?" he whispered hoarsely.

"I don't know," replied Jenny. She gave up paddling and set to work with the bailer instead. She decided that she had never even disliked her husband quite as much as she did Lionel today. In spite of their desperate situation she was actually enjoying seeing him so miserable.

Fortunately for them Abel Baker's small red trawler, registered HH241, was heading back to Barly early that day. He had a good catch already sorted in the hold and the heavy drizzle and thickening cloud heralded very uncomfortable weather to come in the next few hours. With any luck they could get the catch unloaded and into the van and away to Halmouth by teatime.

On board with him were his youngest son John and his wife Sarah. Unlike Charlie's wife Nora, who spent all her time at home cleaning and cooking and knitting, Sarah liked to work the boat with Abe whenever she had the time, or he was short-handed. It gave her a breath of fresh air, she would explain, and as she was almost as useful as a man he didn't mind her coming along. He knew that the other fishermen along the coast regarded this as odd but the arrangement had worked well for over twenty-five years now and he saw no reason why it shouldn't continue for another twenty-five.

He was in the wheelhouse listening to the sweet steady note of the engine while John and Sarah were on deck scrubbing down and stowing the nets. He felt no qualms about being dry while they worked in the rain because he had done the same for his father for years and nobody who worked at sea ever expected to remain dry anyway. The place in the wheelhouse was the skipper's prerogative.

This afternoon he was keeping a careful lookout through the murk for Charlie's and Victor's boats. Charlie had been trawling, like him, and Vic had taken a party of rod-and-line fishermen out to an offshore wreck. They would all be making their way home at about this time. Knowing with such certainty what the others would be doing was all part of the job.

"Bloody fools!" he muttered to himself as he saw the small boat bobbing on the water half a mile ahead. "No right to be out in this weather!" But he knew that holiday-makers were liable to do anything and best kept clear of. Fishing, probably, and for fun too! John saw them and pointed and laughed, and Sarah shrugged her shoulders and laughed too. Then, at the same time as he recognised the colour of the little boat as it rose on the chop, it occurred to him that it was odd that there was no motor on the stern. He altered course five degrees to make towards it.

The two people on board began moving about in an agitated fashion, almost as though some kind of argument was taking place. After a moment a paddle was raised in the air with the blade through the sleeve of a man's jacket. He slid open the wheelhouse door and shouted to John to prepare to come alongside. John was already coiling a line to throw to the little boat and Abe hoped they would know what to do with it when they had it.

When they had brought the cold and angry Jenny and the shivering and weeping Lionel on board they took the boat in tow and Sarah helped the two into the wheelhouse, which became very cramped, and gave them warm sweaters from the bag she kept on board and hot coffee from a flask.

"You should know better, my dear," she said to Jenny, ignoring Lionel.

"I do now," Jenny replied through clenched teeth. "Never trust a man or an engine."

Thomas was hesitant about showing Jenny the letter from school asking if any of the children wanted to join the new ship of Sea Rangers to be formed in Barly. She had been decidely unhelpful about replacing the engine for the boat even when he had offered to pay for one out of his own savings. Altogether she had been a bit snappy lately and rather hostile to any mention of the sea.

"It isn't really a ship you know, Mum," he said, several hours after she had laid the paper aside on her business desk in a corner of the living-room. "It's the shed on the playing field beside Barly Beach."

"Why call it a ship then?"

He thought about it a moment. "I suppose it's because they want us to feel like sailors." Jenny didn't reply and he said, "I'd pay for the uniform myself."

"It's not the money," she said. That was true at last. They were no longer short of finance. "The ship may be ashore but sooner or later they'll want you to go in a real boat."

"Mum, I've been going in real boats for years. Just because something happens to you, you want to stop me. It's you who shouldn't go in boats, not me."

She couldn't deny the logic of this as she reread the letter from the school and such phrases as "teaching the principles of good seamanship at an early age" and "safety on the water" stood out. After all, it would keep him busy one or two evenings a week and several winter weekends when he might otherwise be fussing to take the boat out on his own. So she signed the consent form and Thomas carefully folded the piece of paper and put it in his pocket.

He wondered if he could persuade Jenny to let him have a bigger bicycle to go back and forth between Barly and Innismouth, because he had well and truly grown out of his first one. It would save him a lot of time but perhaps it would cause her extra worry and he knew she had enough to worry about anyway, running a business. After turning the matter over in his mind for some time, and walking to the first two Sea Ranger meetings, he suggested that if they both had bicycles they could go for rides together on fine winter days. His mother seemed to like that idea and at Christmas two smart, refurbished, second-hand cycles were delivered.

Jenny said, "New ones would be extravagant. And anyway, it might just be a phase. We don't know yet if we're going to get any real use out of them."

★ ★ ★

The first sign that the work on the Barly development scheme has begun does not inspire confidence. With a considerable amount of fuss and a certain lack of manoeuvering skill which causes three of the smaller, less impressive yachts on the outlying Sailing Club moorings to be sideswiped, one of them sinking as a result, a pile-driver is brought into the lee of Happy Island on a floating platform and off-loaded on to the beach, where it becomes embedded in the soft sand and is engulfed by the next few high tides.

A daily watch is kept on this by Charlie and Mrs Baker, and Vic and Sam and Jimmy, who retire to the Harbour Inn each evening and during many lunchtimes to discuss better ways of doing the job. They can't understand why the contractors didn't pick a high spring tide to move the pile-driver so that it could be landed directly on to hard sand above the reach of the water. The landlord joins in to tell them that the contractors' men, who also drink at the inn, seem to think that spring tides only occur in the spring, not once a fortnight on the full moon and the new moon.

"They don't know much about the sea at all," he says pityingly, "and even less about our estuary and Barly Beach. Poor blokes. They've just been sent to do a job, they say, and now they realise there are more problems than they thought. They're asking about for someone with local knowledge to advise them."

Charlie shakes his head. "It's always the same with these townees. Thinks they knows it all, then comes asking for help after they get in a muddle."

"They're willing to pay well for some advice," says the landlord. "Quite a lot to someone who really knows their way around the estuary."

"Well, I've got my trawling to attend to," says Mrs Baker pushing her glass across the counter for a refill of Special Brew. "Can't afford to waste good weather."

"Tourist season's just building up," says Jimmy Dog. "Can't take time off from pleasure cruises."

"Besides," says Vic, "A stranded pile-driver adds interest to the sightseeing trips. I think we should leave it there as long as possible."

Eventually, however, the contractors do manage to employ a competent adviser from among the retired naval officers in the Sailing Club and the pile-driver is rescued and put to work on the island, along with several other pieces of noisy machinery which are shipped across with more competence, but no less ado, than marked the first incident. They trample and churn their way across the island, flattening undergrowth and frightening wildlife, some of which is rescued by a team of volunteers from the local school, led by an emotional biology mistress. She tries to enlist the help of the World Wildlife Fund and succeeds in holding up the work for two weeks while boatloads of bird-watchers and scientists descend on the island to assess the situation. Their final decision is that there is nothing special about a few hundred rabbits, and there are no birds using the island that cannot be found in plenty of other locations, so the work is allowed to continue.

Several large trees have to be felled, including one that

still has in its branches the remains of a tree house where a group of children once lived when the island was occupied by hippies.

Thomas sees the trees go. He is working with two of his boatyard employees on board the yacht that is his pride and his largest investment so far, doing some final fitting out before her sea trials. He has known for some time that they would be cut down but he didn't think it would hurt so much and he has to turn away and stare out to the water for several minutes to quell the anger in his heart and the tears in his eyes. His mother was right, as always, but what can he do to help her now?

The ugly racket of the pile-driver at work soon shatters the air across the estuary from dawn to dusk.

"What are they doing?" visitors ask, and those who know explain that they are piling the sand of the island to make a firm base on which to build the entertainments complex. Some of the local people are surprised at the extent of what is being done, and the disturbance being caused, and they complain to their councillors only to be told, "We can't stop it now. It's all been approved. It'll only take a few weeks, you know."

Early one morning Thomas Sharpe and his crew slip the new yacht, which has been called *Silver*, off her mooring and make a record crossing to Roscoff for a boat of her size and class. They don't tell anyone of the time they made and when they return to England a few days later they take the yacht into Halmouth because Thomas doesn't think the moorings at Barly are safe at the moment. He says there are too many people who don't know what they are doing using too small a stretch of water.

SIX

In spite of a promising spring the weather, this last summer in the life of the old Barly, has not been at its best. There have been no long, balmy days and the few holiday-makers with sufficient dedication or foolhardiness to venture out of doors in shorts and swimsuits, rather than sweaters and anoraks, have been more likely to suffer from hypothermia than sunburn. June has produced not a single day without rain and throughout July the west coast has been lashed by gales as one depression after another moves in from the Atlantic. It has been doing no good to the holiday trade or to the engineering works of the Black Corporation. The fishing hasn't suffered though because Mrs Baker will take out her trawler in all weathers and the bigger the storms, the higher the price of fish.

On a night which in any other year would be warm and bright with stars Abel Baker's widow emerges unsteadily from the Harbour Inn with Charlie and Jimmy Dog. They walk together to the quayside and stand in silence watching the water and the sky, noting that the tide has turned and the wind backed round to the south-west, heralding another blow.

THE LIFE AND TIMES OF BARLY BEACH

Along the seafront of Innismouth the coloured lights sway in the freshening wind and a light drizzle dims the floodlight glow of Joshua Brown's Sunways Holiday Camp on the hill above Barly. In the Sailing Club dinghy park all the little boats have been prudently pulled up well above the tide line and the club bar is full of armchair seafarers remembering how it was once, on just such a night, when they were making a passage and managed to battle through against the elements.

The single trawler and three sightseeing launches moored alongside the quay are riding high on the spring tide and they crunch uncomfortably against the stone wall in the swell from which even the harbour wall cannot offer full protection in these conditions. Vic Baker leaves the inn and joins the other three and together they adjust the moorings sufficiently to prevent the boats moving without risking that their vessels will be hung above the water as the tide falls. Charlie Dog feels uneasy as he bids Mrs Baker goodnight and sets off to walk home up the hill with Jimmy and Vic instead of turning into his old cottage. Living in a comfortable bungalow on the new estate is far from convenient for a boat owner who has been used to keeping an all-night watch on necessary occasions.

Mrs Baker checks the moorings again but there is no more that she can do so she retires to bed, knowing that she will wake every hour or so during the night.

The last few drinkers leave the Sailing Club and the inn, slamming car doors, idly kicking the odd tin can around, and calling merrily to one another that perhaps it will be better tomorrow. Gradually the lights go out and all that is left is the whine of the wind and the busy slapping of water against the wall and the boats.

About an hour later a furtive figure can be seen moving along the quayside, looking at the cottages and the inn rather than the water and the sky. The person curses gently as he trips over moorings, then he feels his way along the ropes to the bollards, looking over his shoulder to check that the other ends are those belonging to the trawler.

He is able to lift the first rope clear of the bollard with little difficulty but the next is straining with the full weight of the boat so he takes out a sheath knife, which is neither sharp enough nor large enough for the job, and begins to hack through the strands. He is so absorbed by what he is doing that he hears nothing until the last footfall behind him a second before he is sent sprawling forward towards the edge of the quay by a mighty blow on his shoulders. As he views the black space of water opening and closing between the stone wall and the hull of the trawler he is pulled backwards, swung round, and held by an iron grip at the throat of his clothing, pinned in a sitting position against the bollard.

"Whatever you're doing," shrieks Mrs Baker above the whistle of the wind, "it'll be the last time if you ever try it again! Go and tell your Mr Black that I'll kill anyone who messes with my boat."

She releases her grip and the prowler crawls clear, then gets to his feet and runs whimpering into the darkness, tripping over several more mooring ropes on the way.

Mrs Baker chuckles to herself. "I must have a good case," she mutters as she gathers her dressing gown around herself and climbs aboard the trawler to resecure the cast-off mooring. "They wouldn't risk trying that otherwise! I've got them on the run! They're frightened!"

★ ★ ★

Jenny decided to keep the café open during the winter, for shorter hours than in the summer, because many of the retired people who were making their homes in Innismouth liked to walk along the seafront every day and the café gave them a place to sit and talk or have a bite of lunch before they went home.

Being denied the use of a boat Thomas spent a lot of his time on the trawlers, helping to repair gear and paint things. When the hulls needed scraping and repainting they were beached on the highest tides of the month on Barly Beach. Thomas liked to study their curves which were normally unseen because of the water. He looked closely at the way the steering gear worked and found out a lot about the engines.

Every Tuesday evening he put on his Sea Ranger uniform

and went along to the "ship", which was run by Captain Wragley and Captain Dartman, two brisk little gentlemen with grey hair and clipped accents, who wore very important-looking uniforms and seemed to have spent years of their lives at sea on big ships. They taught Thomas about flags and signals and he spent a lot of time learning the Morse code. Just for practice he used to leave Jenny notes written out in dots and dashes so she found herself having to learn it as well. They were supposed to be taught about tides and weather, too, but Thomas found to his disappointment that they were not told anything he didn't know already.

Almost as soon as the unit was established they began raising money and Jenny found herself involved in jumble sales and film shows almost every month. Thomas organised a bring-and-buy coffee morning in the café one Saturday, with Jenny donating the coffee and other mothers bringing cakes and pots of jam and plants and things they had made.

"I knew you'd be too busy to do any making," Thomas said, "so I thought the best thing was for you to contribute what you normally do anyway."

"Yes, but free coffee!"

"It's not free to the people who come. They pay and the money goes to the Rangers."

"Yes, I get the general idea. After this, could we just keep a collecting box on the counter for people's small change?"

"What a good idea! You really are a great help, Mum."

The object of all this fund raising was the whaler. At first Thomas discussed it in rather loose terms, not at all sure whether it was a full-sized ship or whether they might really be going to chase whales in it. Later he found out it was a big rowing boat, built on the design of the old whaling boats. There was one available from a unit of Sea Rangers along the coast who had recently bought themselves a new and superior model. Captain Wragley said the boat itself was cheap and it came with all its fittings and oars, which was a good thing, but it needed a lot of work doing on it which would be expensive.

"Couldn't we do it ourselves?" asked Thomas as they all sat around in the hut drinking cocoa after a signals session.

Captain Dartman smiled gently. "There's a lot of scraping and one or two planks need replacing, and then there's the varnishing and painting. It's all rather lengthy and specialised, beyond the scope of you lads. Captain Wragley and I would need to do most of it and we just haven't the time. So we think it better to get professional help."

"I can do work on boats," Thomas said. "I've been able to for ages. I could show the others what to do."

It was Captain Wragley's turn to smile. "I don't think you understand, Thomas. It needs more than a lick of paint. Anyway, it's all fixed up with a boat-yard in Halmouth. They're starting work next week."

"When will it arrive?"

"Should be ready by Whitsun. We'll trail it down on the Saturday and have a launching ceremony."

The plan was for the whaler to arrive in the morning and at midday they would gather all the parents and helpers to hear a speech, see the boat christened, and witness something that Captain Wragley and Captain Dartman called "saluting the flag", for which a flagpole had to be erected and painted outside the hut and the boys had to practise marching and saluting. Then the boat would be put in the water and they would have their first row around the island.

"You shouldn't do it that weekend," Thomas said about a month beforehand, after they had practised raising and lowering the Union Jack without getting it stuck. "The tide will be wrong."

Captain Wragley looked at him coldly. He liked to be addressed as "sir" by the boys and Thomas kept forgetting. He didn't like Thomas at all by that time because the boy was apt to argue while the others would just sit and listen to what they were told.

"What do you mean, wrong?"

"It's high tide at ten o'clock, sir. If we start at twelve, by the time you're ready to launch it will be past half-tide."

"That's all right. We can drive the Landrover over the sand to the water's edge."

"After half-tide," explained Thomas patiently, "it's mud, not sand. And it gets very shallow for a long way. There'll only be six inches of water all the way to the channel. And it'll be running out fast. The boat will get stranded." And the Landrover, he thought, but he stopped because the two captains didn't look very pleased.

"It's impossible to begin earlier, unless you expect us to get up at break of dawn to drive to Halmouth."

"Or perhaps you expect us to alter the date of Whit Sunday. I think you'll find, son, that we have enough experience to launch a small boat from a beach."

Some of the other boys sniggered. They regarded Thomas as a know-all and liked to hear him put in his place.

"Sir," piped up one of them obsequiously, "will we be sitting in the boat when you launch it or do we get in afterwards?"

"We'll need most of you to heave it into the water."

"You said full uniform, sir," said another. "Won't we get our socks and shoes wet?"

"I think you'd better bring wellington boots for the actual launching," said Captain Wragley, glancing at Captain Dartman to ascertain that this decision was acceptable. "We don't want to give your mothers extra work, do we?"

They'll get stuck in the mud, thought Thomas, who had lost several pairs of boots that way, but then everything would get rather muddy anyway. He wasn't going to tell them again.

Of course it happened just as Thomas had predicted. All the parents gathered by the "ship" with well scrubbed children and they glowed with pride as the Landrover edged down the hill towing the newly restored whaler. The two captains emerged from the vehicle looking splendid in full white summer uniform and conducted the well-rehearsed ceremony around the flagpole. Jenny had been briefed by Thomas as to what he thought was going to happen and, as she watched the tide receding across the beach while the children were marching and saluting, she could only agree that he was right. She wondered why so many adults found it difficult to listen to the opinions of children. It should have been quite obvious to the two captains that as far as Barly Beach was concerned Thomas was very likely to know exactly what he was talking about.

At last it was time to back the Land Rover and trailer

down the beach to the water's edge, where Captain Wragley and Captain Dartman danced about for some time, shouting instructions to the boys who were slipping and sliding as they tried to push the boat off the trailer into the sea, which was receding so rapidly that with every push towards it there was in fact twice as far to go to reach it. It took a full hour of struggling and commanding and countermanding before the whaler was high and dry on the mud where it could only sit until refloated by the next tide. The Land Rover was so deeply embedded that it had to be rescued by one of Joshua Brown's tractors, which luckily had a winch strong enough to pull it out.

By that time the officers had felt it was necessary to assist the boys in order to save face and everyone, large and small, was equally mud-spattered. They had no choice but to leave the whaler where it was and it was Thomas who reminded them to put an anchor out in case they mis-timed their return.

The parents departed with dirty small boys, minus all those boots that had been bought a size too large so that young feet could grow into them, and were lost forever in the mud.

As they paid Joshua Brown and climbed into the Land Rover Captain Wragley turned to Captain Dartman and said, "Ah well, worse things happen at sea."

"At sea," said Captain Dartman, "you aren't watched by ten small boys and half a town. Your worst mistakes mercifully sink."

After the stranding of the whaler Thomas left the Sea Rangers, or they left him, Jenny was never quite sure which. He could be seen watching them occasionally, on Sunday mornings, as they progressed up and down the seafront or the estuary, according to the tide, with either Captain Dartman or Captain Wragley standing in the stern operating the tiller, impeccably dressed in white shorts and socks and a navy-blue sweater, and shouting "One two, one two!" It would have been quite impressive if the boys had been able to organise their efforts so that all eight oars were either in or out of the water at the same time. As it was, they progressed on their erratic course with all the co-ordination of a demented crab.

Thomas had better things to do. His model sailing boats had reached such a standard of proficiency that they were selling well in the café to the tourists who liked their individuality and their authenticity. But rather than turning out more of the same every year he was ambitious, and keen to make models that really sailed. To do this their sails had to be adjustable according to the wind direction and their hulls had to be well-balanced. He would spend hours on the sands of Barly trying out his boats on the broad, shallow pools left by the receding tide.

Because he was only making them for pocket money he wasn't worried about charging a price to recompense his time so the finished models were sold comparatively cheaply. People would come into the café and ask for boats even when the shelf was empty and before long Thomas had an order book and took deposits. He complained to Jenny that going to school prevented him working on them and asked if he couldn't stay at home. But Jenny said, "It's only a hobby. One day you'll have to earn your living and what you learn in school will turn out to have been much more useful."

"I want to make boats for my living."

"You may think that now," smiled Jenny, "but there are other things in the world more important than boats."

Thomas couldn't think what they were.

During that summer Jenny was preoccupied with expanding her business. The guesthouse next door to the café went up for sale towards the end of the season. It was run down and had been badly managed for some time by the elderly couple who had bought it for a retirement investment and then found that it took up too much of their time. The bank manager was quite willing to advance Jenny a loan that she could repay over eight years, even on present takings, so she bought the place and set about planning to redecorate and refurbish it during the winter months. This made it possible for her to offer continuous employment to the two waitresses and the washer-up she had taken on during the summer. She had to get plumbers and an electrician in as well and for a while the place was in chaos.

Nobody seemed able to get on with their work for very long without calling on her to make a decision or without her being there to watch them. At one point she lost her temper and swore at one of the workmen and to her surprise they seemed to make better progress after that. It encouraged her to be less careful about the way she spoke to people she was employing and she found that if she could laugh and joke with them, as well as swear at them, things got done far more smoothly.

She tried to continue to instil in Thomas the proper way to speak, as she had been brought up, but without any real effect. He had long since picked up the extended vowels and slurred consonants of the Bakers and the Dogs, and some of their more colourful figures of speech too, to Jenny's horror. When he looked at her one day and said, "You're beginning to sound like Mrs Baker or Mrs Sing," she knew that it was time to give up. They were Barly people now and there was no sense in trying to be different.

While the alterations to the guesthouse were going on she felt guilty once more that she wasn't spending enough time with Thomas, though he seemed happy enough as he dashed back and forth on his bicycle, always busy. Next year, she told herself, when the new business is established, I'll take more time off to do things with him. But right now we need the money more. It's security for him, after all.

Working so hard and having food always available she found it impossible to stick to the diet she had set for herself and she tried to come to terms with losing for ever the girlish wispiness of waist and thighs that had always been part of her attractiveness. She knew she wasn't taking enough exercise and this wasn't helped by the fact that she had recently bought an estate car because she found it was cheaper now to go to the newly established cash-and-carry store just outside Halmouth to get her wholesale supplies than to use the delivery service. Once she had the car it was easier to use it even for short errands when once she would have walked or cycled. She told herself that as soon as the pressure of work eased she would go for long rides on her bicycle and reduce her weight by exercise.

Her feet ached with long hours of standing and she always wore flat, sensible shoes. She liked the fashion of maxiskirts that came out that winter and she bought herself two but she found that they tended to be uncontrollable in a gale and she took to wearing jeans or cord trousers most of the time. She kept her hair short because of hygiene with the food.

She had no time at all for men.

★ ★ ★

Lionel Black is not too happy when Commodore Pritchard tells him that he'd like to take the Easterly out for a shakedown cruise along the coast to see how the crew works together. He would be only too pleased to let the boat go without him, even if it means explanations to his father and doing without it for his entertaining for a weekend or two, but the Commodore has assumed that he wants to go along and politely included him in all the arrangements, from which he cannot now extricate himself without losing face.

The Commodore would really prefer to sail without Black because his experience of owners aboard when a boat is being sailed hard has not been happy. If they know what they're doing they want to take charge and the boat ends up with two skippers, often conflicting. If they are novices they become nervous and start demanding that no risks be taken.

The Commodore mutters about this in the Sailing Club bar but not of course when Mr Black is there to hear him. He receives a lot of sympathy from his friends though one or two ask him why he is undertaking the trip if it's going to be so problematic.

"Chance to sail a fine boat, basically," he says airily. "Want to try it out. Thinking of getting one like it myself if it handles well."

Since Lionel is committed to the cruise he has decided to make the best of it. He goes to a smart chandlery in Halmouth that deals more in clothing than in fittings for boats and buys himself a thick Arran sweater and matching hat, big waterproof trousers with shoulder straps, an ocean jacket with a built-in safety harness, all in white, with a pair of yellow wellingtons which all yachtsmen seem to wear. His wife Elizabeth looks at this gear aghast. She is feeling disgruntled enough at having to live in Barly without being abandoned by a husband who appears to have taken leave of his senses.

"But it's midsummer and you're only going down the coast, not crossing the Atlantic."

"I'm told it will be very cold at night and boats can get wet at sea, even in moderate winds."

Elizabeth has been trying to persuade him not to go on this voyage and now she redoubles her efforts. Lionel is not the most exciting man in her life but he is very publicly presentable and he certainly keeps her and the children in the manner to which they like to be accustomed. It would be a pity to lose him.

"I must go," he says. "It's a matter of honour, and good business."

"How can you justify it in the name of business?"

"If I want to turn Barly into an international yachting centre I ought to show an interest."

"An interest is one thing, suicide is going too far."

He points out that far more people die in road accidents than are lost at sea, and a great many people they know have been out to sea in small boats and returned not only safe but exhilarated.

"And sick," she adds.

The weather doesn't look promising on the day designated for his departure but the Commodore says it will soon blow over and they load their gear and six people into Lionel's launch, which suddenly seems very small as it sets off from the bottom of the Sailing Club slipway across the choppy water to the mooring.

Elizabeth watches from the wall, her two children clinging to her skirts, feeling like a Victorian heroine who has been abandoned by a husband in search of greater glories, which, when she thinks about it later in warmth and comfort, is precisely what has happened.

Lionel's time of departure and possible return are both very uncertain so she daren't take the train to London as she often does when he goes away. Instead she collects catalogues and magazines and wallpaper books and plans the refurbishment of the Manor House. Since Lionel wants her to live there he can pay for it to be made habitable. She sends the children to play in the garden where they amuse themselves by inventing war games and lighting little fires.

Meanwhile, tossing about on the mooring, Lionel has successfully stored his gear in the very small space allotted to him. He had thought that spending money on such a large vessel would allow plenty of space for personal belongings but the Commodore has insisted on a lot of additional equipment, such as life-jackets and almanacs and a computerised navigation system. Also he has taken on board a lot of food stores and cases of wines and spirits. Finally there are several sets of new sails. Lionel believed that when his father bought the boat it was basically equipped with all the sails it might need but the Commodore has insisted that in order to race effectively they need at least ten additional sails which all have to be on board now because trying them out is the object of the trip. They take up a lot of space.

When he has stowed his gear Lionel comes into the cockpit and tries not to look at the heaving water. He wonders whether they ought to go with the wind blowing so hard but he daren't mention it. Instead he says, "Right, just tell me what to do."

The Commodore looks at him speculatively. "Go up for'ard and help Bob cast off the mooring while I start the engine."

"Aren't we going to put some sails up?"

"Later, when we're out."

"I would have thought we had enough wind to sail straight away."

The Commodore shakes his head patiently, wondering if the whole trip will be like this. "Wind's on the nose through the river entrance. Can't tack across the bar at this state of the tide."

Lionel doesn't understand what he's talking about, so holding on firmly to every fixed object he can find on the way he walks with as much confidence as he can muster along the considerable length of the deck to where Bob stands on the heaving bows, propped against what looks like a guardrail but is in fact, what Lionel soon learns to call a pulpit. Bob is hauling on a very slippery length of chain that disappears over the edge of the boat and into the water. "Oh good," he says as Lionel appears. "Keep the tension off this for me while I release it from the Samson post."

From this Lionel gathers that he is supposed to take over Bob's position of hauling on the chain. He finds the weight very much greater than he has expected and almost loses his footing on the deck and pitches over the side into the water. After what seems an unnecessarily long time, during which the engine is started, Bob bellows in his ear, "Right! Let her go!" The chain drops into the water where it is held on the surface by a large red buoy with B.I.S.C. painted on it. The bows swing slowly round towards the river mouth and the boat makes careful and controlled way across the bar, where the swell is heavy, and out to sea.

Lionel and Bob return to the cockpit, Lionel deciding that now they are moving walking about is out of the question so he takes to his hands and knees. Back in relative safety he finds that the slime on the mooring chain has made a mess of his new waterproofs but he thinks it may be undignified to make a fuss about this. He has just settled in a corner to enjoy the feel of the fresh wind in his face and the sight of Barly and Innismouth receding astern when he is called upon to crawl along the deck again with Bob, this time dragging a large sailbag, and learn how to "bend on a jib". Then he is introduced to the mysterious difference between halyards and sheets as the sails go up, with a lot of flapping of material and whirring of winches. Lionel always seems to wind these the wrong way, for which the crew appear to enjoy shouting at him.

At last the sails are set and the engine switched off and the motion changes as the boat settles herself at an angle of forty-five degrees, which seems to alarm nobody except Lionel, and cuts through the sea with the leeward rail touching the water. Looking back, Lionel sees that the coast is a mere blur on the horizon and the boat that has always looked so large and impressive on the mooring now seems small and insignificant amid a forest of white-capped waves.

Feeling frightened as well as queasy he goes below and

lies down on his bunk, because he has been told that this is the best cure for seasickness and it is certainly the best way to deal with a horizon that is pemanently at the wrong angle. There he stays for twenty-four hours, only moving to change bunks as the boat changes tack. He is aware of people moving around him and food being prepared and eaten but the only interest his stomach shows is to threaten to leave him altogether. He is stirred finally by the sound of the engine starting and the mainsail being lowered, and he gingerly raises himself and staggers to the companionway and sticks his head out.

"Are we home?" he asks.

"Oh no!" laughs Commodore Pritchard. "We've made Spearmouth."

The boat is motoring into an estuary surrounded by tree-clad hills, much more crowded with moorings and pontoons than the Innis Estuary.

"What a splendid trip that was! We averaged twelve knots. Made five changes of foresail. Pity you missed it, Black. Terrific performance, your boat!"

They all look wet and exhausted with blotchy faces and stubble on their chins. There is a maniacal glint in every pair of eyes and even though it is still early in the day someone is pouring out stiff whiskies and gins.

"Seasickness really got the better of me," Lionel said, having been told that most sailors suffer from it and it's no disgrace.

"Never mind, old boy. Go ashore and have a shower and get a hot meal down. We'll rest up here today and tonight then set off back on tomorrow morning's tide."

When they are ashore, after spending a tortuously long time nosing alongside a pontoon in a marina, Lionel telephones Elizabeth and arranges for her to phone through to the marina office that evening with an urgent summons from his father at their London office. "And send a car down to Spearmouth to collect me," he adds. "I'm feeling very weak."

SEVEN

The time had come for Thomas to transfer from Barly Primary School to the newly formed comprehensive at Halmouth. He wasn't looking forward to the change for two reasons. It would mean travelling for three quarters of an hour each morning and evening on a school coach, and he would be set homework. Both of these seemed to him to be unjustifiable impositions on his time which was already very fully used between helping Jenny, making model boats, and giving advice and assistance to people whose boats needed maintenance and repair on the beach. As his reputation grew these people were more and more inclined to listen to him and even hand over jobs to him and pay him for his work. Jenny began to get used to them wandering into the café and saying, "Is this where that boy lives, the one who's so good with boats? We were wondering if he could just fix . . ."

It annoyed her when they left pieces around the place for him to attend to and, after going on about it to no avail, she decided that the best thing to do was to set aside a large shed at the rear of the guesthouse, which she had used as a storeroom, where all the boat bits could be kept in one place. She thought it was only a passing phase, like the engine had been, and that going to the comprehensive school would give him other interests.

It came as something of a shock to her to find that Thomas had grown up so much already and that they had been here now for nearly six years. And yet in some ways it was as though they had never lived anywhere else.

They went shopping for the new school uniform which was one of the few occasions Thomas had her entirely to himself that summer. Jenny remembered when he had first started at the primary school and she had found it difficult to scrape together enough money to buy him a new sweater and trousers. Now they went to the outfitters in Halmouth and bought everything on the list: all the games equipment, a new bag, an overcoat. Thomas was amazed at how much it all cost but Jenny had the money set aside and she spent it gladly. They piled all the parcels into the car and rounded off the day with a visit to the cinema and a meal in a restaurant. While they were eating Thomas reminded Jenny that she hadn't visited Happy Island for nearly two years.

"I know. I've been so busy. You haven't been over there either, have you?"

"Just the odd trip in other people's boats, showing them the way. There's been so much else to do."

"Has it changed?"

"A lot of litter above the tide line. Too many people who don't care very much."

"I sometimes think nobody cares much any more except us."

"And the birds. We should go there for a picnic before the holidays are over."

"How can we? We haven't got a boat now."

"The happies' boat is still in the shed. I was looking at it just the other day."

"We need an engine."

"I know someone who's got one for sale that would do. Fifty pounds."

"It's a lot of money."

"It would be useful."

"Are you *sure* it works properly? I'm not very happy about it. What if I have another trip like the last one? I think Abe's so fed up with pulling me out of the water he'd just throw me back another time."

"Don't worry, Mum. I'll be in charge. I can get you there and back safely, no trouble."

So Jenny took a rare day off and they went for a picnic. They walked all over the island and looked at the changes in the outline made by violent storms, or unusually high tides. Thomas climbed into the tree house once more, surprised to find that the platform and walls were still intact although the roof had long since fallen away. The engine behaved perfectly but it was a Manners engine, not a Penguin, and to Jenny it seemed altogether more sophisticated. Thomas said that this was so, which meant it was more complicated too, but this one was in good condition and not likely to let them down.

In the autumn after Thomas had started school Myra came to stay to escape from the stresses caused by the success of her book. She and Jenny had kept in touch by Christmas card, Jenny sending delicately tinted prints of a snow-covered Barly or wild birds on the wing, drawn by a local artist, and Myra responding with bold designs based on feminist symbols. She had just completed a second book which had taken her some time because she had also been called upon to lecture at Cambridge, lead international discussion groups and supervise the opening of a women's training centre and feminist library in London.

She looked much the same, just a little more creased about the eyes and forehead, and she might almost have been wearing the same dungarees and shirt as when they last parted. Jenny was pleased to see her because she remembered Myra as having set her off on the road to independence. She gave her one of the best rooms in the guesthouse and managed to summon up the confidence to take the boat and the new engine to go across to the island for a picnic.

Jenny was secretly very proud of her business achievements, and of Thomas's activities, and she wanted Myra to notice how well they had been getting on. She also wanted to share some of the peace of Happy Island with her. But when they were there Myra stomped around with her head down, watching her feet, or threw stones into the sea, and didn't seem to look at what was around her. Instead she talked a lot about politics and women's wages and some council she was on that was being set up to enforce the new equality laws. None of it seemed to Jenny to be nearly so interesting as the daily problems of running her business and she said so.

"It's all right for you, Jenny," Myra said. "You're a capitalist now, in a comfortable position. You remember what it was like when we had trouble finding the money to buy paraffin for our heaters in those wretched little caravans? You've made yourself a cosy niche in a little backwater and you're divorced from the problems of the ordinary woman who's struggling towards expression and independence."

"No I'm not," said Jenny, looking round at the estuary sparkling in a fresh breeze and wondering what was wrong with cosy backwaters. Somebody had to live in them and just because the surroundings were pleasant it wasn't any easier to make a living. "I employ quite a few of your downtrodden women. Someone has to pay wages if anybody's going to earn them."

"You miss the point entirely, Jenny. Your ownership of property is depriving other people. You're letting down your sisters by employing them. You should form a co-operative where you're all equal in responsibility for management and in what you take out for your livelihood."

"I don't think my employees would like to be told that they had to take responsibility for their own work. They seem to be only too happy to be constantly asking me what they should do about things."

"That's because they recognise that you take more profit out of it than they do."

"I think it's because they're not as clever as I am. And they don't work so hard." She was beginning to find Myra decidedly irritating and it was difficult not to be rude. But dealing with customers and employees over the years had given her practice in being nice to people who irritated her, so she just said, "I don't want to be equal to other people, Myra, especially men. I want to be better."

Myra replied, "Competition is against the feminist ethic. Co-operation is the only way forward."

"And it's time to get home to open the bar," said Jenny. She had recently been granted a licence and opened a residents' bar in the guesthouse and it was improving trade considerably, even if it did mean she had to keep an eye on it all the time. Doubtless Myra wouldn't refuse a few free drinks from the hand of a capitalist when they got back. She seemed quite fond of red wine.

They pushed the boat into the water and the engine started perfectly and hummed its way through the water towards Barly Beach. There were a lot of tourists using the beach and Jenny had to pick out quite carefully where they would come ashore through the bathers and inflatables and boats. Amongst them all a spaniel was rushing about picking up sticks thrown for it by its portly male owner. As Jenny steered the boat to within fifty yards of the beach, where she had to think of switching off the engine and tipping the propeller clear of the water before it struck the bottom, the dog owner took the stick from the spaniel and threw it again into the crowded water. It disappeared neatly underneath the boat and was swept into the propeller, twisting and jamming it so that it came to a grinding halt. Jenny jumped into the water up to her waist and grabbed the bows of the boat to pull it the last few yards up to the beach. The spaniel, who had dived beneath the boat to look for its stick, came up on the other side right in front of Jenny and nearly caused her to lose her grip on the boat and fall flat into the water.

As she struggled to regain her balance the man on the beach called, "Oy! You mind my dog, you stupid woman! If you can't handle a boat, don't go out in one!"

"You don't deserve to have a dog, you bloody fool!" Jenny shouted in return. "You've just buggered up our new engine!"

"Typical man!" muttered Myra as she helped Jenny unbolt the damaged engine to carry it up the beach. "Arrogant and stupid!"

"Nonsense!" snapped Jenny as she examined the engine. The propeller and shaft were bent beyond repair and all she could think of was fifty pounds down the drain. "You don't have to be a man to be arrogant and stupid!"

She was right in supposing that Myra wouldn't refuse free drinks and later in the evening, well into her second bottle of rather expensive red wine, she became angry with Jenny, quietly, in the corner of the bar, and began accusing her of being a failure and letting down the cause. Since all their previous discussions had been on a friendly and humorous note, Jenny wasn't sure how to react to this, except to say that she didn't even know she had been supposed to be supporting a cause so how could she let it down?

"Has nothing I've said or written penetrated?"

"Dangerous word, that," smiled Jenny. "Implies sexual domination. Myra, all I'm interested in is making a living to support myself and my son. You're the one who needs penetrating."

To her amazement Myra burst into tears, then picked up the rest of her bottle of wine and went up to her room. When Jenny looked in later she was fast asleep on her bed, fully dressed. She had gone by breakfast-time next morning leaving a note of thanks for such a relaxing holiday.

When Jenny read Myra's next book, not so much out of a sense of loyalty or curiosity as because Myra sent her a free copy, she found there was a chapter called "The Failed Feminist", describing women who were more interested in making money for themselves than sharing their talents with their sisters as selfish and flippant.

Oh dear, thought Jenny, if only I'd known I was trying to be a feminist I might have been more successful at it!

Thomas found the comprehensive school more congenial that he had expected. At first it was all a confusing muddle and he began to think that if they didn't get down to teaching him something sensible soon it wasn't really worth his while to go there. Then one day, walking along a crowded corridor, he saw ahead of him the back of Silver's head. She was taller than she had been of course, and still taller than him, but it was unmistakably her long, dark hair. He tried to push forward to get to her but a big boy grabbed his collar and said, "Get back, squirt!" He saw her disappear into a classroom where he couldn't follow without making a real fool of himself.

He was glad later that he hadn't been able to reach her because when he saw her again and had a chance to study her face he realised it wasn't Silver after all. Her nose was a different shape and her smile was different. But gradually he forgot what Silver had actually looked like and imagined that she had been just like this other girl. He found out that her name was Eileen and that she was three years older than him. He organised his school activities as far as he could so that he could watch her playing tennis at dinnertimes, or be waiting for someone in the corridor when she was due to pass, laughing and chatting with her friends, swinging confidently along clutching her bag of books in the manner that only older pupils could and which younger ones longed to be able to imitate. He never spoke to her, just watched her eating her dinner while he was still queueing, or sitting in classrooms he wasn't going into, or getting into a school bus to be taken somewhere he wasn't going.

He had dreams, though, that one day he would do something really wonderful and she would notice him. Perhaps he would win a cup at sports day, or be mentioned in assembly as having the highest grades in his year, or paint a picture that would be hung up in the school hall so that she would stand in front of it and exclaim, "Who did that? Isn't it marvellous!"

To this end he worked harder than he had ever known he could at everything he had to do and Jenny was well pleased with the reports she received at the end of every term. When people asked how young Thomas was getting on at the big school she was able to say, "Very well. It seems to suit him there. He spends hours doing his homework." And, she thought, he doesn't seem to be obsessed with boats any more.

The spring of Thomas's first year at the comprehensive saw the founding of the Barly and Innismouth Sailing Club, which caused a great deal of interest. The people who had come to live there and kept boats to sail for fun had several good reasons why a club was necessary. They needed showers and toilets and changing rooms near to the water.

They needed somewhere to keep their tenders and outboard motors in safety, and somewhere for little sailing dinghies to be pulled up on the shore in a more organised manner than at present, with everyone just leaving them all over the beach. And they needed somewhere warm and dry to sit and drink and talk and watch the water when the weather was too poor to sail their boats.

A group of yacht-owning residents formed themselves into a committee and elected a Commodore and a Vice-Commodore and a Secretary and a Treasurer and started looking around for suitable premises. There was talk of trying to buy the old sheds on the quay that Abe and Charlie and their families and friends used for storing gear and fish boxes. Those sheds really belonged to the Council which rented them to the trawlermen at a very cheap rate, and the fishing business was still important enough in those days for it to be unwilling to change their use.

The next idea was to buy the piece of land on the estuary end of Barly Beach and build a clubhouse and a boat park and slipway. This made sense because it was next to the safest small-boat anchorage where a lot of the yacht owners had already laid moorings. It was also in an area that the Council had recently designated as building land and it seemed that planning permission would be readily granted. At first the committee members thought the land was owned by Joshua Brown because it was adjacent to the seaward boundary of his farm, but then they found it was owned by a firm called Black Developments, which had something to do with the people who owned the Manor House, and they didn't want to sell. However, they were willing to let it on a twenty-year lease for something as prestigious as a proper sailing club so the committee drew up plans, which were approved by the Council, and asked the President of Black Developments and his son Lionel to be honorary life members of the club.

All these negotiations took several months and were the subject of lengthy reports in the *Innismouth Herald*. It was autumn before the foundations of the new clubhouse were laid by Mr Rufus Black in an impressive ceremony. Abe and Charlie sat in the corner of the Harbour Inn public bar and talked about how they were going to form a club too, since it was obviously going to be impossible to put out to sea without a membership badge.

In the same year as the foundations of the new sailing club were laid a firm of builders, called *B.I. Developers*, began to level the land on the side of the hill overlooking the point between Barly and Innismouth, and put up new bungalows. They were very smart little houses, according to the drawings in the windows of the new estate agent, *Boxes*, that opened in Innismouth High Street. They were offered with ninety-five percent mortgages, arranged through the local solicitor's firm of Box and Baffle. They attracted people from the Midlands who had been to Innismouth for a holiday and wanted to retire there, and some people from Halmouth who wanted to live further from the growing city and could afford to run fast cars to get to work on the improved arterial road.

Victor Baker's wife, Louise, persuaded him that it would be much nicer and safer for the children if they lived on the hill, away from the quay, so Victor scraped together the depoist money, with the help of Louise's father, and bought one of the first few houses to be started. The building society wanted him to have a regular job before they would let him borrow money so he followed his brother Sam into the employment of the Council, as a delivery van driver for the Supplies Depot in Halmouth. This actually earned him less money than running the pleasure launch for four months of the year so when the following spring came he gave up his council job and returned to his boat and nobody in the building society or the solicitor's office seemed to notice.

When he and Louise finally moved into their bungalow it all looked so nice that Jimmy Dog and his Annie, who was expecting their first baby, decided to follow them "up the hill", as the people in Barly were calling the new estate. Jimmy got a job as a milkman, which was available because the dairy was extending its round to cater for the new houses. He worked out that if he got up early enough in the summer he could keep the job and run his boat as well.

Bearing in mind Lionel's advice, which by this time was the only good thing about him, Jenny bought both the cottages on the quay that had been vacated by Victor and Jimmy. They were next door to each other and cheap because of their short ground-leases which had only twenty-five years to run. She paid cash for them by increasing the mortgage on her boarding house, which had doubled in value since she had bought it. She had the cottages given a quick coat of fresh paint and let them to holidaymakers.

Thomas didn't think this was a good idea. He thought that it would be nicer to live there themselves because Barly was more interesting than Innismouth and much more convenient for boating activities. But Jenny said they were quite comfortable in the flat above the café and the cottages were an investment. "I can keep a better eye on the business here," she said. "It's either a question of you cycling back and forth or me, and you've got stronger legs."

She hadn't used her bicycle much, just for an occasional dash out to a local shop when the town was full of holidaymakers and car parking was difficult. As Thomas grew out of his he began to use hers, with the saddle as low as it would go.

* * *

Abel Baker's widow has for some time now been an increasing cause of embarrassment to the Harbour Inn at Barly. She has been a regular customer there for a long time, ever since she first came to live in one of the quayside cottages. They have always regarded her as eccentric, being a serious sea-going woman, but harmless. Over the years she has come to drink and swear more and more, but usually under control and with good humour. There have been occasions, of course, when she has become uproariously inebriated and has had to be carried home by her fellow trawler owners, but these have been rare and therefore forgivable. She is known to be caring to her friends and clever enough to score points against enemies. Most people who know her refer to her as a good sort, or an old harridan, depending on whether or not they like her.

But recently, since Charlie Dog left his cottage, she has been drunk almost every night and she sits and mutters to herself in the corner or buttonholes people at the bar, both known and unknown to her. She pours out to them the details of her quarrel with the Black Corporation, whom she regards as being the instigators of the court case against her, despite the fact that Innismouth Town Council is named as the plaintiff. She hints about grudges incurred years ago, before she married Abe, when she was trying to make her way and refused to be put down by people who considered themselves to be important. She makes wild accusations, too, about paid hooligans tampering with her mooring lines and even trying to get aboard at night to open the seacocks.

People shake their heads and exchange the view that she's lonely, poor thing, since Abe died and the other cottages are empty. They listen to her because she belongs in Barly but they look forward to the day when the court case is over. Then, they think, she will have to go. How can she win, poor woman? She may be right but the Council is the Council and people shouldn't be allowed to get away with defying its orders. Otherwise, where will it end?

The pile-driving has stopped, though only for the time being according to Mrs Baker who knows the island well and has always said that they can't build anything much there without going deep into the sand. A dredger has dug out part of the beach on the estuary side of the island and a line of concrete pontoons has been rafted up to make a jetty where barges come alongside almost every day to unload machinery and steel bars and cement and . . . sand.

"Sand!" exclaims Charlie Dog. "Ain't there enough sand there already?"

And people who know about these things explain kindly to the old man that sea sand isn't any good for reinforced concrete buildings. They have to have clean, graded sand from the quarry near Halmouth.

"No doubt at a good price," says Mrs Baker who knows that the quarry is owned by a subsiduary of the Black Corporation. Neither has she failed to notice that the barges that bring it along the coast have *B.C. Transport* painted on their sides.

These facts are also commented on by correspondents to the *Innismouth Herald*, who keep up a flood of letters protesting about the noise caused by the building developments and the disturbance to the users of the estuary. James Box is worried by these letters but although he has dropped hints to the editor, the paper continues to print them. Apart from problems with his own popularity, he thinks there might be an increase in public support for Mrs Baker if the facts of the case become known. He has heard rumours of a midnight attack on Mrs Baker and her boat and he shudders at the thought of the Blacks employing thugs for such tactics. Out in the open that sort of thing could ruin him.

He wishes he was still handling the case so that he could advise going for a settlement out of court, with an increased cash offer and more generous concessions for the fishing boats to use the marina eventually.

He tries to contact Rufus Black in his London office and is told by a secretary that Mr Lionel Black is now handling all business connected with the West Country development from his house in Barly. He tries to make an appointment with Lionel and finds that he is temporarily unavailable, owing to being involved in some yachting trip along the coast.

EIGHT

"I'm going to build a boat this summer," Thomas said.

He had carefully picked Sunday morning to announce this, knowing that they would have a little more time to talk because Jenny had made a rule that she should have Sunday mornings off once Thomas was at secondary school and she saw so little of him, what with his travelling and her increased business commitments. She looked up slowly from her newspaper, thinking about this announcement, then said, "We've got a boat. It's an engine we're short of."

He shook his head. "I'm going to build a sailing boat so we won't need an engine. I've decided we have too many problems with engines so I think sails may be better. I've sent for the plans and Abe and Charlie say I can use the shed to work in. I've got most of the tools I need but I'll have to buy the wood and the fittings." He didn't think it necessary to add that he hoped building and sailing his own boat would impress Eileen. In the Easter holidays he had seen her with her parents on a cruiser, picking up a mooring just off Barly. Of course she hadn't noticed him, but it had set his mind working once again on the model boats he used to make and he had decided he knew enough about it by that time to try a real one.

"Who's going to pay for it?" asked Jenny.

"I think I can manage. I've got quite a lot in my Post Office account. But of course if you want to help . . ."

"Do you know how to sail it when it's finished?"

"I've got a rough idea. But it would be nice to have some lessons. Do you know they're taking on an instructor at the Sailing Club this summer?"

Jenny had heard. She looked at Thomas's bright face and strong hands and knew that nothing she could say was going to stop him. "I'll pay for the lessons," she said. "And perhaps I could learn too. It's time I had a hobby away from the business."

"Great!" said Thomas. "You'll love it, you really will!"

Jenny doubted that more and more as the days passed. Nothing that had happened to her during the last few years had done anything to reduce her fear of the water. She had suggested taking lessons as a way of postponing the scheme to build a boat, which she could only see as ending in disappointment because she was sure it would turn out to be more than Thomas could manage. She had decided to join in because that might help to alleviate her persistent guilt that she never did enough with Thomas. It might also convince her that he really was quite safe on the water. She booked up the lessons for a week during the Easter holidays and arranged to take time off.

She was relieved when the first day of the course turned out to be in a classroom, or at least in the social room of the Sailing Club which was doubling as a classroom while the courses were being run. The one thing she was really worried about was being in one of those unstable little boats that people seemed to point in some random direction according to the way the wind was blowing, and which appeared to have no means of stopping other than running into something. A bit of theory first seemed like a good idea. On the other hand Thomas was impatient. He understood the theory and wanted some practice. He only sat and listened carefully all day because Jenny had paid for this, and because he knew she needed to be reassured before they went in a boat.

"Good morning," began the instructor. "My name is Wallis. First lesson is parts of a boat." He pinned up a huge diagram on the wall in front of them and gave them small printed copies for themselves. He was tall and muscular, with blue eyes and longish blond hair. His face was regular and square-jawed and when he smiled, which was often, staring directly at someone for an instant before pasing on to the next thing he was saying, he showed an impressive array of straight white teeth. His tanned body was covered with a downy layer of golden hair that glinted as he moved his fine limbs, to which he treated everyone to the maximum view by wearing open sandals, short white shorts, and a white shirt unbuttoned to his navel. The picture was completed by a gold medallion on a heavy chain that nestled in the little tufts of hair on his chest.

Jenny tried hard to concentrate on the diagrams of boats for a full hour while Thomas helped by prompting her when she was asked questions and by explaining the connections between things, until he was told to be quiet and listen. There seemed to be a hundred new words to learn and when she asked Wallis why everything had different names to what they would be called ashore he said, "So that we can distinguish them from one another," which seemed reasonable until she realised that everything, everywhere, was called something so that it could be distinguished from something else.

She had barely had time to come to this conclusion when the coffee break was over and they were sitting in front of the blackboard again. Jenny would have liked to ask the instructor more questions but he was occupied with two of the other students, leggy, athletic-looking girls with long gleaming hair tied in bunches and neat tight behinds barely covered by shorts made of cut-down jeans. They giggled and fluttered their eyelashes and already seemed to know a lot about sailing. The other two students were men, one large and beefy and middle-aged, the other young, pale, and nervous, wearing glasses.

Wallis began again, covering the blackboard with increasingly incomprehensible diagrams while he spoke. "Now this is the wind and this is your boat, with your sails set at right angles to the wind like this, and the helmsman sitting on this side of the boat so that the wind is coming directly over the beam, except that it feels as though it's coming across at an angle because of the difference between the actual wind and the apparent wind of the boat's forward motion. This point of sailing is called a beam reach and it's the easiest and also the fastest point of sailing. It's the safest as well, because you can easily manoeuvre in either direction by pulling the helm towards you and letting out your sail and thus bring the wind further astern of the boat, on to what we call a broad reach, or by pushing the helm away from you and sheeting in your sail and coming on to a close reach, and eventually on to a windward beat. If you come too far in this direction you luff up and the boat's forward motion stops because the sails won't fill when they're pointing towards anywhere within forty-five degrees of the wind. That means you have to tack, or go about, which I'll show you how to do later, and bring the boat round on the other tack, travelling at a ninety-degree angle to your original course. If you bear away from the wind further than a broad reach you come on to a run, with the wind directly behind the boat, and the sails goose-wing, like this. If you want to change direction so that the stern of the boat goes through the wind you have to gybe, bringing the boom across to the other side of the boat like this, and then you can manoeuvre around the other side of the wind circle back on to a close reach on the other tack. When the wind is behind you and the boat is on a run, then you're being blown along. When you're sailing to windward the boat is being sucked along and in order to prevent the boat being blown sideways as it's being sucked forwards, you have a centreboard which you lower into the water, to different depths according to your point of sailing: right down when you're beating, half when you're reaching, and right up when you're running, because then you need as little as possible hull resistance in the water."

Thomas stared at the blackboard in amazement and the

two girls yawned. The large man wrote frantic notes on a pad and the other man took off his glasses and polished them, muttering "Interesting!" every now and again.

"Any questions?" asked Wallis giving a cursory glance over their heads and smiling at the two girls. "No? Right, I'll go over that once more, then we'll have lunch."

The afternoon was spent on something called a "simulator". The two girls called it a "stimulator" which they thought was very funny and which kept them giggling throughout most of the lesson. It consisted of a mock boom with the lower part of a sail attached to the mock stern of a boat, with wooden seats on either side to represent the sides of the boat on which the helmsman sat. Attached to the end of the mock boom was a real piece of rope, which was called a sheet.

Wallis gave them another incomprehensible talk, and then a demonstration, and they all had to practise pushing the tiller and pulling the sheet, and changing hands and stepping across the boat calling "Ready about!" and "Lee-o!" at the right moments, which none of them could do. When they all in turn collapsed into a heap in what would have been the bottom of the boat, Wallis roared with laughter and told them to do it again, and said how lucky they were he had this clever simulator because if they were in a real boat they would have capsized it by now, which did nothing to reassure Jenny.

Eventually Thomas and the two girls got it right, and the young man with glasses made a passable attempt and they all had a cup of tea, during which Wallis held what he called a "debriefing" which consisted of shooting questions at them all about what he had told them that day. None of them was certain of any of the answers but he just laughed and said, "Never mind, it'll all make sense when you're in the boat."

"When do we get to be in a boat?" asked Thomas.

"Tomorrow, if the weather's kind. In the morning we'll learn to rig and de-rig and in the afternoon I'll take you all out in pairs."

Taking them out consisted of putting them into a sailing dinghy two at a time, with the sails rigged, towing them in a boat with an engine that he called the safety boat, and which Thomas later renamed the danger boat, and when they were in an area of water clear of moorings and the tideway, releasing the towrope and shouting instructions about what to pull and push and what the crew should be doing. This time he was dressed in a bright red knee-length wet suit, unzipped low enough in front for his medallion and hairy chest still to be on view. He fitted all his pupils out with life-jackets, insisting that they were necessary, which soon became obvious, though Jenny wondered why they seemed to have been specially designed to severely restrict her agility in the boat and therefore make it even more likely that she would end up in the water.

First the two girls went out together and managed to complete a few manoeuvres accompanied by glowing praise. Their success reassured the other four waiting on the Sailing Club slipway and the two men were taken out next, giving each other nervous glances.

As soon as they were let off the tow the boat careered through all the points of sailing in quick succession and then heeled over and capsized. Wallis drove the danger boat round them in slow circles, shouting instructions which neither of the pupils floundering in the water seemed able to assimilate. In fact after a while they began shouting back at him so he took the boat in tow still floating on its side in the water, told the pupils to hang on to it, and pulled them slowly and ignominiously back to the slipway. There in shallow water he supervised them pulling it upright and bailing it out before telling them to go inside and have a hot shower and change their clothes. Then he turned to Jenny and Thomas and said, "Your turn."

"No," said Jenny, "I don't think . . ."

"Come on, Mum," said Thomas, pushing her ahead of him into the boat. "This is what we've been waiting for. I'll helm first and you crew."

"No," said Wallis. "I think your mother should take charge of the boat first."

"She's nervous," Thomas explained, "and I know what I'm doing."

Wallis glared. He had tried to ignore Thomas, and this

usurping of his authority was more than he would have allowed in most circumstances. But it had been a bad afternoon and he just wanted to get it over with and keep his date with the two girls. A quick capsize with a child at the helm who had insisted on taking charge couldn't possibly be construed as being his fault, and it would serve the dual purpose of convincing the boy that sailing was not yet within his grasp and bringing an end to the afternoon's proceedings.

Thomas got the boat sailing and concentrated hard, carefully telling Jenny how to crew as they tacked, and how to let out the sails as they changed course so that the wind pressure didn't blow the boat over.

"Now change places!" shouted Wallis from the danger boat.

They did so, again carefully. Jenny, trembling, felt the boat leap forward in her hands, straining against the tiller and the mainsheet. Again Thomas told her what to do and apart from being very clumsy, and moving too fast when they tacked, she found she could manage. Thomas showed her how to slow and stop the boat by letting out the sails, which Wallis hadn't mentioned to anybody, so that she began to feel in control. She suddenly realised that in a real boat, with real wind, messages came back to her through her hands when she was doing the right and wrong things.

She was enjoying it so much that they went too far up the estuary and Wallis in his danger boat came alongside and impatiently told them to make their way back. "Do you want another turn?" Jenny asked Thomas, ignoring the instructor. Thomas nodded and they changed places again. The danger boat came close on their windward side and even Jenny realised that they couldn't tack to get back to Barly whilst he was there. Wallis waved his arms at them, letting go of the controls, and the boat veered towards their dinghy. Thomas shouted to Jenny to mind her head and pulled the tiller towards him hard. The boat made a turn through a hundred and eighty degrees, away from Wallis, the boom slammed across, and they were sailing safely in the other direction with Wallis in the danger boat taking some time to turn and catch them up.

"You gybed!" he shouted when he was alongside again. "I haven't shown you how to gybe yet! What the hell do you think you're doing?"

Thomas and Jenny declined to reply and fortunately at that moment the instructor was in no position to insist on their attention as he was having to concentrate on driving his boat through the moorings. They sailed back to Barly and Jenny helped Thomas to de-rig the boat, her knees shaking so much that she wasn't sure she could stand up much longer.

The following day the two men didn't turn up. Jenny thought twice about it, wondering if they wouldn't be safer hiring a boat on their own and letting Thomas teach her all that he had picked up. But they had paid, as he pointed out, and an instructor like Wallis must be able to teach him something he didn't know already.

"Of course," mused Jenny, "we haven't actually seen him sail a boat yet, have we?"

Nor did they. For the next two days they suffered more lectures in the mornings, about wind and weather and tidal flows, and de-capsizing—a little late, as Thomas commented. Every afternoon they rigged two of the Sailing Club's boats and put out on the estuary. Thomas and Jenny were in one, completely ignored by Wallis. The two girls were in the other, constantly circled by the danger boat and given instruction and encouragement.

On the last day they took it in turns to perform manoeuvres and sail in triangles and de-capsize a boat deliberately turned over, in order to gain a certificate. Thomas and the two girls performed faultlessly. Jenny was nervous and fumbled and fell when she tacked, and nearly capsized the boat when she gybed, and had to make six attempts to come alongside a mooring buoy. When they were ashore the instructor congratulated the two girls while he wrote out their certificates, then turned to Thomas and Jenny.

"You're quite good, young man, but unfortunately you lack finesse as yet. Of course, you're too young to be awarded a full certificate. I suggest you come back for more practice and take the test again next year."

Thomas looked disappointed but he swallowed and asked, "What about my mum?"

Wallis shook his head sorrowfully. "Well of course, if she'd concentrated and given her full attention to what she was being taught she would have come out better. But it's a known fact that some people will just never make sailors however hard they try. It's especially difficult as you get older. Your reactions slow up, I'm afraid. You're just not suited to it, Mrs Sharpe."

For the first time in her life Jenny felt middle-aged. She knew she had let herself go, overeating and not taking enough exercise, and not worrying about whether her clothes were particularly smart. But it came as a shock when someone like Wallis referred to her as "getting older".

I'm not thirty-two yet, she thought. I suppose that seems old to Wallis, but am I really slowing up? I can still rush around all day and do my job in half the time it would take most other people. What's the matter?

That evening she took a walk up the hill past Joshua's farm to the top of the cliffs and found herself very out of breath.

She made a resolution to eat less and walk more. She even thought of making more of an effort to ride the bicycle regularly, though she would have to buy Thomas a new one of his own if she was to do that.

Once she realised that Thomas was really a most competent sailor Jenny bought him a small second-hand dinghy that he could manage on his own and let him loose on the water. More than that, she went with him as often as she could and he taught her to sail with confidence and an increasing amount of skill. They would often tack back and forth watching Wallis in the danger boat shouting at his pupils or fishing them out of the water.

"That man," said Thomas, "is a case of terminal prat."

"I hear he's very good with the girls," commented Jenny. Wallis's reputation was spreading.

"But can he sail a boat? That's what I'd like to know."

As Jenny had hoped, the sailing set back Thomas's plans to build his own dinghy. He was content to enjoy the summer on the water and leave the building until the winter.

When he was sailing he found that he didn't think of Eileen so much, though he always kept half an eye open for her.

Once she gained confidence Jenny wanted to spend more time sailing with Thomas than she was organised to spare from the business. She decided it was time to put a manager in the flat above the café and move herself and Thomas into the cottages in Barly. She engaged a builder to knock the two cottages into one and install some new plumbing and some central heating. Thomas had been right, Barly was a more interesting place to live in than Innismouth and she became quite impatient to be nearer to the boats.

She advertised the job of café manager and spent some time interviewing suitable applicants and weighing up the pros and cons of their likely honesty and reliability, and whether they would be able to get on with all the customers. Finally she made a decision that was wholly subjective, remembering her own state of life eight years before, and offered it to a young woman with a degree in business management who had a daughter, five years old, and no husband. She continued to run the guesthouse herself, though she now had a cook and a general assistant working for her and her job consisted of the overall organisation of bookings and accounts, and opening the bar in the evening. She bought Thomas a new bicycle so that she could have her own back and travel quickly between the cottage and the business, whatever the state of the holiday traffic.

The cycling didn't help her to lose weight. It increased her appetite and built up her leg muscles.

★ ★ ★

Black the Elder considers that Lionel entering the Easterly for the Baltic Race and actually going to sea in her is taking his instructions too far. The vessel represents capital investment on the part of the firm and it is meant for the entertainment of business associates, not for chasing about at the mercy of the winds and tides. And Lionel, too, represents a valuable commodity to the Corporation, taking into account his training and the connections and expertise he has built up.

The matter is discussed at some length over a formal

family Sunday lunch at the Manor for which Rufus Black has flown from London in his private helicopter. The lunch is meant to have been an elegant buffet on the lawn but turns out to be a huddle from the rain inside the verandah, with the adults finally retiring to the drawing-room and the children in front of the television for the afternoon.

Elizabeth is wary but gratified to find that for once her father-in-law is taking sides with her against his son. She has long considered wide open spaces to be unhealthy and if they are filled with huge quantities of water they become downright dangerous. When she has said so for the sixth time both men become impatient with her and Lionel snaps, "I know all that, and anyway I've no intention of going on another of those masochistic jaunts. But the boat is entered now and I can't let the Sailing Club down. It'll mean a lot for the development of Barly and Innismouth to have a boat in the race, specially one that might even win."

"All right," concedes Black the Elder. "But make sure the insurance is adequate."

"And then there's the regatta."

"Which regatta?" chorus Elizabeth and Black the Elder.

"The Sailing Club. It's the fifteenth anniversary of its opening this summer and they plan to hold a regatta. The little dinghies will race around the island and the big yachts will race up the estuary, then out to sea and round the bell buoy and back."

"And when will this be?"

"September, I think. You must remember laying their foundation stone."

Black the Elder shrugs. "I lay so many, most of them more important than little sailing clubs."

Elizabeth knows that the real purpose of his visit is to enquire into the progress of the work at Barly, and that she must absent herself during this discussion to save Lionel the humiliation of possibly being reprimanded by his father in front of her. She would like to go around the garden and gather a few choice blooms in an idle and ladylike manner—she has bought herself a new flat wicker basket for this purpose and never used it yet—but it's raining again so she settles down in front of the television with the children to watch an old cowboy film.

In fact, today Black the Elder is not displeased with his son. It is he who has to be on the defensive when Lionel points out that the pile-driver is now lying idle, waiting to begin work on the causeway across the bar. They can't start on the island end until a special Act of Parliament has been passed to allow them to close a waterway previously in public use and they can't start on the harbour end until Mrs Baker and her cottage and her trawler have been removed. Black the Elder has been assured that the parliamentary business was dealt with before the summer recess, due to the pulling of some far-reaching strings, and all they await is the paperwork. That should be in their head office any day now but they can't afford to be seen to proceed without it in case there are any repercussions from the matter of the fishermen's cottages.

"What about Mrs Baker? Haven't we got her on the move yet?"

"Not exactly. The case is due to come up in the next County Court sessions but the Council hasn't been given a date yet. How's the rest of the work going?"

"We've demolished those old storage sheds on the quay, though that was a bit dicey in law according to Box. The shop is closing at the end of the month. All the other cottages are empty."

"Can't you knock down all the cottages except hers?"

"I asked the demolition manager about that. He says it might be possible but he couldn't guarantee hers won't fall down as well, because they're probably all holding each other up. If we do it accidentally we've got real trouble on our hands. And that doesn't get rid of her trawler moored just where we want to begin the causeway."

"Does she still sell her fish?"

"Several stone a day, I believe, to the fishmongers in Innismouth."

"Can't that be stopped?"

"There is a demand for fresh fish. We could buy in from further away and undercut her price but people would notice the difference. Tourists expect fresh local fish when they come to a place like this."

"There must be ways of getting rid of a trawler."

"There are, but she's a sly old baggage and people are afraid of her. Best thing would be to kill two birds with one stone. Get rid of her and her trawler at the same time. I"ll give it some thought."

NINE

Jenny believed that the Bakers and the Dogs would resent her making improvements to the cottages and coming to live there, because she knew how suspicious they were of outsiders in their community. In fact she found that what they had resented was her letting them to holiday-makers whom they found to be something of a nuisance, tending to stay up late and hold noisy barbecues on the beach, often misjudging the tide so that they would be frantically cooking sausages and steaks as the water lapped around their feet. They would grumble, too, about the seagulls and the smell of fish, and from time to time one of them would fall into the harbour and have to be rescued.

By comparison Jenny was a long lost friend and was welcomed wholeheartedly. She had visited them of course, and they had called in to her café when they were in Innismouth, but it hadn't been like the early days when she had lived in the caravan and walked past every day, and had scandalised them by taking on a building labourer's job. On the other hand they felt they knew Thomas well because he had never stopped hanging around Barly and talking to them and having cups of tea and cake in one or another of their homes. Thomas, bowling down the hill on a bicycle or carrying pieces of boat up the beach, was part of their scene.

While they were moving in Sarah Baker and Nora Dog made tea and helped Jenny to unpack boxes and commented on how tired she looked. They thought a change would do her good. A proper home of her own and time to relax would soon put her right.

"You've been working too hard," said Sarah, putting down a tray of tea and fruit cake on a packing case.

"I've had to get the business on its feet. I need the security for Thomas's sake."

"Nice boy, Thomas," said Nora, plump and overalled, standing in the doorway. "But you're well set up now, my dear. You need to take things easier."

"This cake," said Jenny, sitting down and munching, "is amazing! Proper fantastic, as Thomas would say! I suppose he often does!"

"Every time he has a piece," smiled Sarah.

"He's a bright lad," said Nora.

"This moving house is making me so hungry. May I have another piece, just to keep me going? Do you like this wallpaper?"

"Not quite to my taste," said Nora. "A bit too modern. I go for them flowers. What young Thomas needs is a real father and you at home to look after him."

Sarah shook her head and glared at Nora. "A mother staying at home don't necessarily make the place any happier. Wouldn't necessarily improve Thomas. I like that blue colour on the other wall."

"Thomas has a father already," Jenny said firmly, having heard hints of this nature before. "He's never been much good to us. We don't need another one."

"You're right there," chuckled Sarah. "Lot of bother on two legs. What colour will you do the kitchen?"

The move to Barly was very convenient for Thomas. During the winter, partly in his bedroom in the cottage and partly in the sheds on the quay, he built his boat. He steamed and glued and hammered and screwed, and took bits off and put them back again until finally he was satisfied with the hull. Jenny said, "I thought it was a complete plan you'd bought. All set out for you. Why do you keep changing your mind about bits of it?"

"I'm modifying it as I go along," Thomas replied. "The buoyancy tanks and the front bulkhead weren't really efficient."

Eventually there was the smell of varnish and paint in the shed and a mast and a suit of sails were ordered, which Jenny agreed to pay for since Thomas's efforts in actually finishing the boat seemed to merit some tangible reward from her. One day when she went in to admire the progress and remind Thomas about tea time and homework she saw that he had painted a name on the stern, *Sharpeshooter I*.

"That's neat," she said. "But why 'One'? There isn't a 'Two', is there?"

"No, but there will be. I'm bound to think up improvements when I've sailed her a bit. I was thinking, I'd like to race this boat. Do you think I could join the Sailing Club?"

"They won't like it when you win," Jenny commented jokingly.

"No they won't, will they." Thomas's reply was serious. "Perhaps they'll ask me to design boats for them so that they can beat me."

"Thomas, you won't have time. Not with going to school and doing your own sailing."

"Oh, I don't mean now, this year. I mean later, when I've left school."

★ ★ ★

Everyone in Barly and Innismouth who knows anything about the daily comings and goings of the boats is more than surprised at the sight of HH241 stranded on the far end of the main beach of Innismouth, well clear of the estuary. It has been put ashore on a small stretch of sand that is uncovered at half-tide, between two dangerous outcrops of rocks that lie just below the surface of the water. It's a very exposed position because there is no protection from the swell running from the sea, and it's directly in the main current as soon as the next tide rises. When trawlers are beached for scraping and painting it is usually on Barly Beach or sometimes on the island. Of course, it's impossible to use the island now but there's only one trawler left anyway. Why wasn't it put aground on Barly?

Not many people watch the actual grounding because it happens early in the morning, soon after the trawler has put out from Barly harbour. As it proceeds down the channel, parallel to the main beach, it can be seen to develop a definite list and before it has even made the open sea it turns in a wide circle and begins to edge between the rocks on to the beach, only being kept on a straight heading to clear the rocks by skilful use of engine and steering.

As soon as the boat has settled on the sand Mrs Baker throws out a stern anchor, then runs two over the bows, one of which she buries firmly in the sand, the other she passes round a convenient lamppost and hooks over the wall of the main promenade.

A watching traffic warden says anxiously, "I don't think you're allowed to do that."

"Allowed? *Allowed?*" shouts Mrs Baker, even more dishevelled than usual. "You go and find your council employers and get them to tell me I'm bloody not allowed! I'm here till the next tide, and that's that!"

The traffic warden watches her stomping off along the pavement, her sea-boots squeaking and spurting water out over the tops with every step. Head down, hands deep in pockets, she grows smaller and smaller as the straight line of the promenade swallows her up. The warden looks again at the anchor and peers over the wall at the trawler. He is an Innismouth man and knows you don't cast adrift the mooring of a boat, so what can he do about it? Write out a parking ticket? He glances at his watch and makes a note of the time in his little book, then goes on his way.

"You've put it on the rocks, missus," says one of the policemen who is on the beach an hour later, poking and prodding at the hole in the planks on the bottom of the hull. "You shouldn't have brought her so close. If you'd stayed out in the channel you'd have been all right."

"If I'd stayed in the channel I'd have bloody sunk, you fool! I only brought her in through the rocks to beach her because the pumps couldn't hold the water down long enough to get back."

"Well," says the policeman, "if you'd already gone out and was on your way back, you must have done the damage out at sea. Was you fishing over a wreck, perhaps? I don't see that this is any of our business."

Mrs Baker's eyes are glinting dangerously. She has had several neat whiskies in the bar across the road whilst waiting for the police to arrive and she is in no mood to be told she doen't know what she is talking about.

"I ain't been fishing at all today," she says slowly and carefully, as though talking to a child. "I put out to sea, came along the channel, and noticed that the pumps was working extra hard. Next thing the steering's getting sluggish. I pop down into the hold to see what's happening and it's half full of water and I can see it's coming in a hole. Holes let water into boats, in case you don't know. And the bigger the hole, the faster they sink. Now that hole's not a very big one, else she'd have sunk at the quay. It's a smallish hole, especially designed to let me get out to sea and then sink, and it can't have been made all that long ago. You got to ask around Barly and see if there was anyone suspicious hanging around early this morning."

The policeman scratches his head. Once it would have been easy to do as she suggested but between workmen and holiday-makers Barly seems to be full of suspicious characters all day long. "I can't see," he says, "that anybody would hack a hole in your boat, missus. I still think you hit something, coming out of the harbour perhaps?" He looks at the expression on her face and takes into account the fact that she must have taken HH241 in and out of Barly many hundreds of times and adds, "No, perhaps not."

"If you'd stop talking and have a look for yourself," she says, "you'd see quite clearly that there's a difference in appearance between a hole made from the outside and one made from the inside, and this hole was definitely made from the inside."

"It's true," says a voice and Thomas's serious face appears through the hatch leading into the hold. The rest of his long body follows and he scrambles over the bulwarks and drops down on to the beach beside them. "The damage was quite definitely done from the inside. A good piece of planking has been chopped at, probably with a sharp axe or an iron spike, and it must have been quite difficult to do."

"Is this your professional opinion, sir?" asks the policeman, relieved at last to find a third party he can rely on, particularly as it's a man. "Would you be prepared to make a statement to that effect?"

"It is and I would. But first I must organise a gash repair so that the boat can be taken up to Barly. She can't be left here once the tide rises. She'll go on the rocks."

"Really, sir, I'd rather you made a statement and left the boat as it is until a police photographer gets here. You're destroying evidence otherwise and it makes it difficult if we should come to bring a case."

"How long would the photographer be?"

"Couple of hours, I reckon."

"Don't you know anything about tides?" shouts Mrs Baker, jumping up and down and pointing at the water, already moving back up the strip of sand towards the trawler. "The boat's got to be looked after first. I have to get her off. Come on, Thomas, get your hammer and nails out."

Thomas walks up to his van, parked on the promenade, in which he carries all the necessary emergency equipment. The second policeman, who is older and wiser than the one who has been doing most of the talking, nods to his colleague and says, "You get on with looking after your boat Mrs Baker, and perhaps you and Mr Sharpe will drop into the station later to make statements. We'll just have a little look around and make a few notes while you're working."

It doesn't take long to patch up the trawler so that it can be taken up to Barly on the next tide and beached there for the damaged plank to be properly replaced. It doesn't take long, either, for the story to circulate around all the bars and shops in town, with admiring comments about the quality of Mrs Baker's seamanship, her having the nerve and the skill to take the trawler into the gap between the rocks when many lesser skippers would have lost their boat altogether. It does take rather longer for Mrs Baker to calm down and sober up. When she has got rid of her hangover the next day she goes into the police station only to be told that it won't be necessary for her to make a statement. The police have decided that as the evidence was removed before a proper examination could be made, they won't be able to bring a case even if they do catch the culprit, if there ever was one.

Mrs Baker isn't surprised at this turn of events, knowing the way the Blacks go about things. The only way she'll see any justice is to organise it herself. She begins to hatch a counter-plot against the person she knows is responsible. "I'll get him in court," she promises the listeners in the Harbour Inn, "you wait. But I'll get him anyway, just to make sure."

Meanwhile Thomas Sharpe loses a lot of sleep, sick with worry as he turns the situation over in his mind, knowing that Mrs Baker could well have lost her life on the trawler. Finally he telephones the solicitor in London who dealt with Aunt Patrick's will for his mother, and invites him to visit the seaside.

★ ★ ★

People who stayed in Jenny's guesthouse would watch the sails in the channel and the estuary and ask where they could have some lessons while they were on holiday. Jenny hesitated to direct them into the clutches of Wallis, who was now beginning his third season at the Sailing Club, still busy convincing people that they were too stupid or uncoordinated to manage boats. She asked Thomas if he thought he could take some pupils out at weekends and in the holidays. After all, he had taught her to sail quite competently. Thomas was only too pleased because he knew he could do a better job than Wallis, and he needed to be busy.

During the summer term Eileen had taken her exams and left school and now it seemed a dull and empty place to Thomas, full of loud voices and bad-tempered teachers and scruffy books with increasingly difficult work in them. He felt sorry for himself because Eileen had never loved him in return for his devotion, but then how could she? She didn't know of his existence. He had never even plucked up enough courage to send her a Valentine card. Then one evening when he was sitting on the harbour wall staring at Happy Island and feeling particularly sad, Jenny arrived back from work on her bicycle and saw him. She left the bike on the quay and came over to sit beside him. "What's the matter, Thomas? Why so sad?" she asked, and she put an arm around his shoulders and gave him a hug.

This severely embarrassed him because he thought he was too old to be hugged by his mother. He had avoided allowing her to come so close for some months now. He pulled away and glanced over his shoulder to make sure that nobody who could possibly take word back to school was watching. "It's nothing. I'm not sad. Just watching the water."

"Yes, that makes me sad too." She sighed, wondering how Thomas could have grown up so quickly. She missed the small boy that she used to cuddle.

Thomas turned to look at her face and saw a tear in the soft wrinkles at the corner of her eye. He thought that perhaps he had hurt her feelings. After all, she was his mother and he was supposed to look after her. If he didn't love her and hug her, nobody else would. There was nobody else in the world to love her except him.

Suddenly he felt very ashamed of having been ashamed to be seen being hugged, and he flung both arms around her. "You're the most important person, Mum," he said, "and this is the most important place." And he meant it.

For the rest of that summer term he couldn't get back home from school fast enough in the afternoons. He would even have liked to take days off but Jenny wouldn't allow it. He was often to be seen on the water in his *Sharpeshooter*, but he soon found it was too small for taking pupils so when the holidays began Jenny sold the first little boat she had bought him and invested in a second-hand *Traveller*, a sturdy class of dinghy that could be used for teaching two or three people at a time.

At first the customers were anxious at being taught by such a young instructor but he appeared competent and they liked his method of taking them across to the island for lunchtime picnics and talking to them about the sailing and the estuary while they sat on the sands drinking beer and munching sandwiches. It made the whole frightening experience much more fun and they went away satisfied and generally able to handle a boat. On her free afternoons Jenny would take out *Sharpeshooter* by herself and meet them and sometimes take one of the pupils on board with her to give them more practice. Before the summer was over bookings for the guesthouse began to come in for next year specifically from people who wanted to learn to sail. Jenny considered buying another *Traveller* and engaging a full-time instructor.

Being out on the water so much made Jenny's skin brown and leathery, with deep creases around her eyes where she screwed them up against the sun. The sailing and the cycling made the fat on her thighs harden into powerful muscles. Her wrists became very strong and her hands were even more calloused than when she had been a builder.

She laughed a lot, specially with her friends the Dogs and the Bakers. Because sailing made her so thirsty she took to downing pints of strong ale at a remarkable rate for a woman.

TEN

The pile-driver begins work again, this time on the side of the island that extends to meet the sand-bar. As they pile, they build a platform from which the next row of piles can be driven and the whole structure gradually creeps out into the river. There is some difficulty because at first they don't drive deep enough and the very strong spring tides push the piles from a neat upright line into a random bent edge, rather like a row of crooked teeth. Lionel Black curses and dismisses the engineering foreman and engages a man with better qualifications who commands a higher salary but undertakes to get the job done without further mishap.

People in the Sailing Club come to realise that the new development will mean the channel between the island and the harbour will soon be closed to them, and the only way from Barly to the open sea will be the long way around the other side of the island. They mutter angrily to the Commodore who tells them that the plans have been available in the Town Hall for months now to anyone who cared to ask to see them.

"It's a bit late for objections at this stage, old boy!

Anyway, the causeway will give the anchorage more protection and when the marina's built you'll have a far more comprehensive service, you know."

Charlie Dog sits on the harbour wall, puffing at his pipe and watching the work. "They'll never close that channel against the tide," he opines. "Narrower they make the gap, faster it'll run. You mark my words."

But the only person listening is his friend, Abe's widow.

Old Mrs Sing actually cries as she closes down her shop for the last time. There is no ceremony. She has sold off almost all her stock to her neighbours and her old customers, and on a rainy summer evening she pulls down the old-fashioned shutters and locks and bolts the glass-panelled doors. She goes back into her living-room to continue packing her china and ornaments in readiness for the removal men who will be arriving in the morning. They have told her that they will do the packing as part of the job but she doesn't trust them with her best bits and pieces. She has lived and worked here for forty-five years and she has a lot of bits and pieces. She wonders how she will fit them all into the new place.

Soon there will be a supermarket in Barly for the residents and the people who use the marina and she was given the option of taking over and running it. But the rent seems very high and she thinks it's time to retire. She has put her compensation money into buying one of the bungalows on what is still known as the new development, even though it's well over ten years old now, and she plans to grow flowers and visit her grandchildren.

The day after she moves out a demolition gang moves in and within a week there is nothing left but empty space and rubble.

Charlie Dog watches it happening and wonders if it's really necessary. He walks down to Barly nearly every day, either to sit in the Harbour Inn or on the quayside. It's a long way for an old man, specially the uphill climb back, but he knows that it irritates Chrissie to have him sitting around the house all day. Besides, he misses the beach and the boats, the capsizes and collisions, the shivering children digging endless channels to the water's edge, and the sight of the parents who seem so intent on disposing of their offspring that they push them out from the beach into the tideway in inflatable rubber boats.

Once the members of the Barly and Innismouth Sailing Club realise that their fifteenth anniversary regatta will assume special importance as the last time they will be able to hold events using the channel across the bar, or launch their dinghies from the slipway on Barly Beach, they plan to hold a water festival and a special parade of decorated boats, as well as the usual races.

In the bar of the Harbour Inn Mrs Baker has suggested that the pleasure-boat owners ask if working boats can join in the parade and when this is approved by the committee she asks Charlie Dog if he can get his old trawler back into the water for the parade, for old times' sake.

Charlie's trawler has been laid up on Barly Beach for the past year while he looks for a suitable buyer but it's an old boat and he isn't looking very hard. At the thought of putting it in the water again his eyes gleam. He works out that he can launch it on next week's high tide and starts to give it a fresh coat of paint. Mrs Baker asks him if his trawling gear is still in working order.

"Oh, I don't want to bother with that," he says.

"Would be nice, though, being a working boat, to be able to show how the gear works. People will be interested. If they've watched the parade from the seafront they may come round to the harbour when we've finished and want to see. After all, these are the last working trawlers from Barly. They're of historical interest."

"You're right," says Charlie. "Maybe they'll even want to make a telly programme about us." He wonders why his friend is so keen to take part in an event that stands for everything she's been shouting against these last months. "I've only got old nets, though." She must be up to something that she isn't giving away yet.

"Never mind. No doubt they're still fit to catch a sprat or two."

When he next visits Barly, towards the end of August, Rufus Black is more than pleased with the progress of the project. His son seems to have learned at last that it doesn't pay to skimp and offer second-best salaries when you need to hire men who know what they're doing.

He takes a trip himself across to the island in the site manager's launch and inspects the foundations that have been laid for the leisure centre. It always looks well for the President of a Corporation to be seen to be taking an interest in mundane details. It impresses upon the minds of the workers that there are people in charge who are interested in more than collecting the profits.

He wants to be sure that the Barly and Innismouth regatta won't interfere with the building of the causeway, and Lionel assures him that this is unlikely. "We can't close the gap anyway until after the big tides in September. It's scheduled to be finished by the end of November, before the really bad weather sets in."

"Good. Good. By the way, the Baker case is due to be heard early in October. I got word yesterday."

"Splendid," says Lionel. He can't wait to be rid of that woman. She has been a disturbing influence on his life for far too long. Now he's heard that she's even going to have the effrontery to parade her trawler up and down the seafront in the coming regatta.

★ ★ ★

When Jenny advertised for a professional sailing instructor she was worried about ending up with a duplicate of Wallis, so she let Thomas interview the applicants because he had a far better idea of the sort of questions to ask that would determine whether they knew what they were doing or not. Five people responded to the advertisement. There were two unemployed P.E. teachers from Halmouth, both of whom did look like potential Wallises, except that one of them was dark and swarthy. There was one retired army officer who lived in a village further up the estuary and said he wanted some activity to keep him occupied during the summer months. There was one grizzled, suntanned, bearded man who said he had just returned from five years of teaching sailing in the West Indies. And there was a girl who was waiting for a place at university, tall and slim, with long dark hair which she wore in a single plait that hung down her back to her waist.

Jenny invited them all down to Barly separately for a morning or an afternoon and she and Thomas met them and talked to them on the quay, then Thomas took them out for a sail. When the last one had come and gone and they were sitting together over supper, Jenny said, "I thought Major Keyes might be the best bet. He knows the estuary."

Thomas shook his head. "He's too structured. Shouts orders at people. Doesn't use his tiller extension properly. Says they didn't have such things when he learnt to sail."

"Oh. Who do you think then?"

"The girl, Maureen."

Jenny was surprised. "Isn't she rather young and inexperienced? What about the man from the West Indies?"

Thomas shook his head again. "He kept asking about safety boats and whether there was any deep-sea fishing hereabouts."

"And the other two?" But Jenny knew what the answer would be.

"Can't sail boats, not properly. They think they can because they can make them go in the right direction, but they can't set the sails according to the wind and they know nothing about the tides."

"And Maureen knows all these things?"

"Spot on. Honestly, she knows what she's doing."

"Well, if you're sure, I'll write to her."

"Good. I already told her she's probably got the job, subject to your approval. And she can't travel back and forth from where she lives on the other side of Halmouth so I suggested she could rent a room here or in the guesthouse."

This time Thomas fell in love because he liked the girl. Of course, if Maureen hadn't been able to sail and hadn't looked like Silver he wouldn't have noticed her in the first place, and to begin with he did think of her as "that girl who looks like Silver". But before long the most attractive things about her were that she could sail a boat well, she laughed a lot, and she liked him, in that order.

For Thomas that summer became almost as magical as the one spent on Happy Island ten years before. The weather was perfect and when he and Maureen were free of pupils in the evenings or at weekends they would sail off together in the *Sharpeshooter* and rediscover the island, or explore quiet little beaches and coves further up the estuary or along the coast that Thomas only half knew about.

It was in this way that he found the derelict fish cannery at Innstone, two miles up the river from Barly. Here for years, in more prosperous times, the Barly trawlers had unloaded their excesss catches which had been tinned and sent away by rail. There had been a branch line from Halmouth, a siding right into the factory, and a deep-water quay. When the numbers of trawlers operating out of Barly had decreased as small boats became less efficient, the cannery had closed, followed by the railway. All that was left now was a partially silted-up channel, the weed-strewn quay and three large empty sheds, stripped of machinery but still in sound condition.

The first time thay landed there, nosing in carefully at high water through the weed that choked the channel and trying to avoid the lines of two small boys who were fishing from the quay, Thomas knew he had found what he was looking for. They tied up the boat and wandered around in and out of the sheds, looking at things, watched anxiously by the young fishermen who were accustomed to being interrupted now and again by couples seeking privacy but had never seen anybody arrive from the water before.

"What an absolutely perfect place!" exclaimed Thomas as they stood in the middle of the largest building.

Maureen glanced doubtfully at the cracked patches of broken glass. "It's a bit basic," she said. "Not very comfortable. Perhaps one of the smaller rooms—or if we walk a little way along the river bank."

"Of course it needs a lot of work." Thomas was almost talking to himself. "And the channel would need to be dredged . . ."

"Thomas, what are you talking about?" By then she had spent enough time in the company of this attractive boy, who looked at her longingly with his intense blue eyes, to have grown used to his mind being on other things than her, especially when they were sailing. But she had really thought that today, at last, he was looking for somewhere more private than a beach so that they could go further than chaste kisses and hand holding.

"I'm talking about my boatyard. I wonder who owns this?"

Maureen decided that nothing would happen unless she took the lead. She said, "Do stop thinking about boats, just for once," and she put her arms around him and gave him the sort of kiss that she knew from past experience would arouse any young man in love.

"What are you thinking of?" he asked, still only half-aware as she stopped for breath. "What's more important than boats?"

She led him to the most secluded corner she could find and spent the rest of the afternoon showing him. It was after that afternoon that the camping began.

Thomas looked out the little tent that had somehow never been returned to Mrs Sing and told Jenny that as the nights were so perfect he and Maureen wanted to camp out on some of their evening trips. Jenny had noticed the dark velvety skies and the glowing moonlight on water bathed by soft warm breezes, not without wistfulness, and she said, "Yes, Thomas, that sounds nice," and thought, perfect for what? Should I be making a fuss about this?

"What if the wind changes and you don't get back in time for your pupils in the morning?"

"We'll plan our trips according to the tides so we'll always be able to get back somehow." And they did.

"And if a gale blows up?"

"We're supposed to be instructors. We can sail the boat in a gale." And they could.

"What if you've had an accident on the water and I won't know about it till morning? How am I going to explain to the rescue services that my schoolboy son and the sailing instructor often spend the night out together?"

"If it'll make you any happier," said Thomas, "I'll buy one of those small packs of flares so that if we *are* in distress we can draw attention to ourselves." And he did.

Jenny noted that he didn't volunteer not to stay out if it would make her any happier and she left it at that. Perhaps

I'm being an irresponsible parent, she thought, but they're young and happy. They're happier than I ever was. Why spoil it for them?

In the autumn Jenny was summoned to Thomas's school for a parents' meeting. There was nothing out of the ordinary about this. It happened at least twice a year and she would dutifully queue up to talk to teachers, all of whom always told her that Thomas was making good progress, really was a bright boy, working hard. In spite of his busy life at Barly he seemed to get all his studying done and whenever Jenny asked him about this he would shrug his shoulders. "If they gave me more to do I might find it difficult. But there's no point in telling them it's easy. I mightn't have time to do it properly if they gave me more."

But this particular parents' evening was different. At the end of the school year Thomas would be able to leave and the headmaster wanted to explain to the parents what their children could choose to do next, though after listening to Thomas's teacher telling her about A levels, and engineering courses, it seemed to Jenny that it was more a case of informing the parents what it had been decided their children should do.

Jenny talked it over with Thomas. "Yes," he said, "they are rather hooked on this engineering line, like it's flavour of the year. We've had people coming to the school to talk about it. Everyone who's good at physics is going to be an engineer."

"They say you have the right sort of mind," Jenny told him. "Enquiring, practical, problem solving—all that sort of thing."

"I don't deny it," Thomas said, "and it will be useful when I leave."

"You can't leave without knowing what you're going to do."

Thomas smiled patiently. "I did tell you, Mum. I'm going to build boats."

"Oh yes!" Jenny laughed. "But that was ages ago, like being an engine driver or a policeman."

"Not like being an engine driver or a policeman. Boat-building is specialised. It takes a lot of knowledge."

"I can see it's an absorbing hobby but can you earn your living at it? Surely there's not that much call for new boats?"

"If you enquire," said Thomas, "I think you"ll find that it's a growing market. More and more people have money to spend and leisure time to spend it in."

"What kind of boats do you intend to build?"

"More *Sharpeshooters*, Mark II. And perhaps something larger if I can break into that market."

"I suppose you think you've only got to hit upon the perfect design and the world will beat a path to your door?"

"It has been known to happen."

Jenny became irritable. She didn't like it when Thomas disagreed with her and she had to assert her authority. It made her feel middle-aged and grumpy.

"Well I think I must insist that you get a proper education before you embark on these schemes. After all, you've only got one chance. You must stay at school and take your A levels and then think about professional training. Meanwhile, if your boat ideas work, that would be nice."

"I agree with you about the education," said Thomas with a pleasant smile and Jenny relaxed. "I've already looked into it. I've written to the boatyard in Halmouth and they're offering four apprenticeships next year. I've got an interview next week."

That winter, before Thomas left school, they paid for the fine summer with an early spell of unusually cold weather. It was a damp, grey, numbing cold and soon after Christmas Sarah Baker caught flu, followed by an attack of bronchitis, and she seemed to just fade away. Everyone had thought of her as a tough old woman in spite of her small frame—she must have been, mustn't she, to have raised those boys and worked with Abe the way she did?

Jenny went to visit her each evening and noticed how clammy and humid was the Baker's cottage compared with her converted pair with their damp-proofed walls and central heating. Sarah wouldn't stay in bed but was sitting in front of the kitchen range with a scarf wrapped round her neck, coughing and spluttering with frustration as she watched Abe and John preparing the tea, not at all to her satisfaction. Then one day she didn't get up at all and Abe said if she wasn't any better tomorrow he would call the doctor. During the night she coughed and spluttered herself to death. John ran round to Jenny's to phone an ambulance but by the time it arrived it was too late.

The odd thing was that Nora Dog, who had always been large and healthy, followed the same way within a week. Jenny thought her illness must have been started by grieving for her friend, and perhaps not eating properly at the same time as picking up the same virus. She suggested this to Mrs Sing as they stood together in a corner of the churchyard at the funeral, to which everyone in Barly and its surroundings seemed to have come.

"Oh no, dear," said Mrs Sing. "It's just that they did everything together, all their lives, you see. From being babies they lived next door, went to school together, started work in the bakery together—that closed down years ago—got married on the same day to Abe and Charlie, had their first babies in the same week. Couldn't keep them apart, you see. They had to go together. I bet they'd have liked a double funeral if they could have got it spot on. Pity they put Sarah away before they knew Nora was going."

Jenny looked at Abe and Charlie standing stoically beside the grave, their ruddy faces stiff and unemotional, and thought it was awful that they had to go through this experience twice in such a short time. Behind the two widowers their families sniffled and fidgeted.

"Look at them," whispered Mrs Sing. "Poor things. Wishing they'd done more when they could and wondering how on earth they're going to manage looking after the old fellows."

But the old fellows didn't seem to need looking after. As soon as the funeral was over they changed into their working clothes and put out to sea single-handed in their trawlers. At first Jenny thought it might be some ritual suicide she was witnessing but by evening they were both back with fine catches of herrings which they landed and packed before going to the Harbour Inn for their pints.

ELEVEN

Maureen had promised to come back the following summer in her university vacation to do more sailing instruction but in May she wrote to say she was travelling abroad with a group of students and wouldn't be able to work for Jenny after all. She sent her love to Thomas and wished them both well. By this time it was only what Thomas had come to expect of people who said they would return, and anyway he was preoccupied because he had to begin his apprenticeship in Halmouth as soon as he left school in June so there was no long summer holiday for him.

Early every morning he left on his small motorbike and didn't return until almost six. It was still light enough then to go sailing, of course, but most pupils wanted to be home and having their tea by that time. He could only teach at weekends, and did, but that left Jenny all week with two spare boats and a queue of pupils, and no instructor. So she contacted Major Keyes, the ex-army officer who lived up the estuary, and found him still able and willing to help out. He kept the pupils happy but, as Thomas had said, he was very structured, keeping mostly to the same area of water near to Barly and not taking people for picnics on the island unless they specifically requested it, and then declaring it to be a waste of good sailing time. However, he was successful at teaching people to sail, which was the important thing.

Eventually, because it seemed as though it would be years before Thomas had much time to devote to instructing again, Jenny sold Major Keyes both the *Travellers* and from then on sent her customers to him, thus providing the service without having to worry about organising it.

A lot about Barly felt different that year. Not only was there no Thomas readily available to go sailing or to mess about repairing bits of boat in the shed, there were also no Sarah and Nora with their fish and their gossip and their criticism of one another. Sam's and Vic's and Jimmy's wives took it in turn to visit and clean up and cook meals for the "old fellows" but they were always too busy rushing back to their own families to sit around and talk over a cup of tea. Jenny took to making tea for Abe and Charlie, and going out to talk to them if they docked their boats before she had to go over to Innismouth for her evening's work supervising the bar and restaurant.

When the boats were moored and before they unloaded the catch, they would sit for ten minutes or so on upturned boxes or coiled nets with their steaming mugs and swap stories about what they might have seen today that was new or remarkable, or listen to Jenny telling them about the latest doings of the holiday visitors. At first Jenny found the smell of fish at such close quarters almost nauseating on a warm afternoon and she worried in case it should cling to her clothes the way it did to Abe's and Charlie's. She always tried to dress up smartly for the evening part of her job and more than once she had arrived at work to find a streak of tar or fish scales on an almost new crimplene dress. She wore a lot of crimplene because it was easy to launder.

The holiday-makers came and went in their fortnightly routine and to them Barly appeared the same. There were still pleasure launches and trawlers and wide expanses of sands at low tide, and sailing lessons. The Harbour Inn still served a good pint and decent bar snacks. And for rainy days there was always Innismouth just a step away, with its cafés and amusement arcades and the new sports centre that had just been opened.

Because Thomas's spare time was in the evenings and Jenny's in the afternoons, she took to going out sailing alone when she wanted to relax. Whenever the opportunity arose she and Thomas still went out together but sometimes they hardly met for days on end. The ideal boat for single-handling was the *Sharpeshooter* and sometimes people watching thought it strange to see a sturdily built middle-aged lady rigging and sailing off alone in a racy-looking little dinghy. But they would be told, "Oh, that's Jenny Sharpe. She's all right. She knows what she's doing on the water."

The concentration and exhilaration of wind and water took her mind off any stress and worry about her business, which she found was more difficult to control now that she wasn't living on the spot. She was beginning to ask herself if she needed to work so hard. Thomas wasn't earning very much but he had offered to pay for his keep, an offer which Jenny refused since he had bought his motorbike and his working clothes and tools out of the money he had saved from his boat repairing and sailing instruction. But he plainly wasn't going to need her financial support for much longer and then she would have only herself to provide for. Her properties alone were worth twenty times what she had paid for them. If she invested the money she could live quite comfortably on the income. But what would she do? Go away for a long cruise? What was the point of being anywhere else but Barly? And if she was in Barly she might as well work. Sitting and watching boats all day might be entertaining for a while but not for the rest of her life.

Perhaps one day Thomas really would build a wonderful boat and they could sail it around the world. But by that time he probably wouldn't want her along any more. What young man dreams of going on a romantic voyage with his mother?

She thought about this while sitting in the little office at the back of the café, going through stock and account books. Being back in her starting place always made her feel nostalgic, and angry too of late. She was becoming increasingly aware of a drop in takings and a sloppiness about the way everything was done. The manageress was off duty for the afternoon, having gone out with her little girl and her boyfriend, whom Jenny suspected was an unofficial husband by now. When she came in, not having announced her plans to be there that afternoon, the two waitresses had busily changed all the table-cloths and Jenny sensed that if she hadn't appeared the job might not have been done, though it was supposed to be part of the daily routine and she had installed an automatic washing machine so that they could be laundered easily. When she had managed the place, even before she had bought it, she had never taken short cuts on cleanliness and service.

She watched through the half-open office door as an elderly couple came in and sat at a table near the window. They ordered tea from a waitress, a plump, clumsy girl who seemed to fall over something every time she moved and who took several minutes too long to attend to them considering that there were few other people in the place. While they were waiting for their tea they kept looking around hopefully, as though expecting a friend. Jenny noticed that they said little to one another, as was often the way with older couples, but they were holding hands under the edge of the table and every now and again their eyes met and they smiled gently.

When their tea arrived they spoke for some time to the waitress who then came to Jenny in the office and said, "They old people is asking to see you, Mrs Sharpe." She smiled, a wide and friendly smile that was her saving grace as a waitress.

"Me in particular, or the manageress?"

"What they asked for was you. That is, if you are 'little Thomas's mum'." The friendly smile changed to a giggle, then a snigger as she went into the kitchen.

Jenny wondered if there was a complaint. But it turned out that the couple had met in the café some years ago, while on holiday, being served with tea by "little Thomas". They had visited each other often in the meantime, finally setting up house together.

"But that didn't seem right, you see," said the old lady. "We've always tried to keep in step with modern ideas, but it just wasn't the same. So last week we got married and we've come here on our honeymoon. We thought we'd like to tell you."

"That's wonderful," Jenny said, trying to remember which summer it was that they had been amongst the hundreds of customers. "I hope you'll be very happy."

"Oh, we are. It's different when you get older. There are so many anxieties when you're young."

They smiled into each other's eyes again.

"I'll tell Thomas. I'm sure he'll be pleased. He's at work at present."

"Work? My goodness, hasn't time flown! He was such a lovely little boy! What's he doing?"

"Learning to build boats."

"Of course."

Jenny went into the kitchen to see if there was any special cake she could offer as a treat for the occasion and to tell the waitress not to charge them for their tea. The plump girl was still sniggering, sharing a joke with the other waitress who was rather more slender and considered herself to be very sexy.

"Ain't it funny, missus?" said the plump girl, nearly dropping a pile of plates she was removing from the dishwasher.

"Funny?"

"Yes. Them old people. Behaving like a couple of youngsters when it's obvious they're past it. Getting married just to hold hands in front of the fire."

"If that's what they want and they're happy about it, why is it funny? And what makes you think they're past it? Sex isn't the prerogative of the young, you know. Your equipment doesn't wither away when your hair turns grey." Jenny found a pretty iced cake and set it on a plate before she turned back to the open-mouthed waitresses. "Furthermore, you two shouldn't be out here gossiping when there are customers waiting."

The plump girl immediately dropped the teapot she was holding, whether out of shock or spite Jenny didn't know but there seemed no good reason for it to have suddenly hurled itself to the floor. As she crossed the kitchen back to the service door she said, "And if you break another piece of crockery in this place it'll be your last. I won't be able to afford to employ you any more."

After serving the old couple she went back to her job in the office and not long afterwards she heard the two waitresses still gossiping but this time at the counter, watching the customers, instead of the kitchen. The plump girl was complaining, "I can't help it, you know I can't. Things just slips out of my hands." This made Jenny think that perhaps the girl was in the wrong job. There must be work she could do where dropping things didn't matter.

The thin girl said, "Don't worry about it. She's just a jealous, frustrated old baggage anyway."

Jealous of them?

Frustrated? Well, sexually frustrated perhaps, but when had she had time to worry about men during the past few years—when had she found one worth worrying about anyway?

Baggage? A bit overweight, true, but not clumsy with it. But old?

I'm not old, she thought. I'm hardly even middle-aged, not forty yet. It does seem a long time though since I was their age, fresh out of school and my mind full of clothes and hairstyles and young men, in that order. The strange thing is that I feel just the same now as I did then.

But Thomas has grown up and Barly had changed. Something must have happened to me.

★ ★ ★

Jonathan Harty, the solicitor, who isn't all that young any more but who is far more prosperous and successful than he used to be, remembers with a certain wistful fondness the bright young woman with dark hair and a small boy who inherited Lady Patrick Mallory's capital and very cleverly invested it in a business that she could run to support herself. Once the matter of the will was completed there was no need for further contact. In the intervening time he has married sensibly and said all the right things to the right people and become more and more important in the legal world.

THE LIFE AND TIMES OF BARLY BEACH

A letter from a young boat builder in the West Country mentioning a familiar name and a Barly address brings back a memory of an evening spent with Jenny in a London hotel, which seemed quite innocent at the time but which he later often thought might be construed as unprofessional conduct with a client. He replies to the letter saying that of course he will see what he can do to help, for the sake of old associations, but before he visits Barly he would like to look at the papers relevant to the case. Thomas sends him a lot of photocopies of summonses, deeds, Acts of Parliament, local by-laws, letters and newspaper reports, together with a succinct summary of the course of events so far.

Harty writes to Box and Baffle, slightly bending the truth by saying he has been engaged by Mrs Baker to represent her, and asking for their papers on the case. He spends a long time studying them, then telephones Thomas and makes an appointment to travel to Innismouth to see him. He decides to combine the trip with a little break for his family and books a week in September in the Marine Hotel on the seafront at Innismouth. The hotel is usually full at that time of the year but because of the poor weather this season they have had several cancellations—the kind of people who stay there have money to spare to go to the Mediterranean instead. They are pleased to be able to offer one of their best suites. Being a successful man the solicitor does not quibble about the cost. After all, most of it will be allowable against tax.

It is the week before the Baltic Race and Thomas knows he will be busy on his boat, but the time must be spared.

It is also the week of the Barly and Innismouth Sailing Club anniversary regatta.

James Box is alarmed when he is approached by Harty's firm and he reports to Lionel Black and his father the news that Mrs Baker has engaged a London solicitor to fight her case. He is asked to visit the Manor House where Lionel has his office and he sits uneasily in the big room that makes his own office look small and poky by comparison.

"That'll cost her money," says Lionel. "Why has she done a thing like that?"

"Because she's worried that she might not win after all," suggests his father. "Someone's told her that if she pays well she can get the verdict she wants."

But James Box has other thoughts. He knows that important London solicitors don't take cases unless there's a good chance of winning. Lost cases, however fat the fee, do reputations no good. And the fees are high, there's no doubt about that. If Mrs Baker wins the Town Council will have to do the paying.

"I think," he says to the Blacks, "we ought to ask for a private meeting with this solicitor and see how he feels about settling out of court."

"We've always been ready to settle out of court," says Lionel, "but the stupid woman won't admit she's wrong."

"No, I didn't mean asking her to settle. I meant offering her a settlement. After all, it's not just a matter of money, is it? She's not asking for increased compensation. She's after stopping the development altogether. And we can't afford that, can we?"

The father and son exchange glances of doubt for the first time. It hasn't occurred to either of them before that money may not be enough.

★ ★ ★

Jenny clung to the upturned remains of the hull of Thomas's *Sharpeshooter*, wondering firstly what had happened and secondly what she was going to do next.

It had been a spectacular accident. The wind was strong, but nothing that she hadn't managed before, and she had been sailing just outside the estuary mouth on a rising tide, amusing herself by surfing the boat on the waves that were breaking over the bar. She knew it was a dangerous occupation but she had done it many times before, both alone and in Thomas's company. She saw what she thought were some twigs floating ahead of her in the water, then too late realised that the twigs were attached to a fairly large branch. The boat hit the branch, broached across the surf and rolled over, part of its hull ripped out. The mast stuck fast in the sandy bottom near the bar and while it held

Jenny managed to scramble on to the wrecked hull, pulling herself up by means of a sheet and a lot of adrenalin.

Several waves broke over her and the boat, then the hull became detached from the mast, losing more of its bottom in the process, and began to be carried by the tide towards Happy Island. The surf was breaking hard on this side of the island and Jenny knew that once she was caught in it the boat would be quickly pounded into small pieces and she might be turned over and knocked out on the bottom, stabbed by splinters of boat, or dragged down by the undertow. None of these possibilities appealed to her.

There was a large green navigational buoy about a hundred yards away, marking the main channel around the island. Thomas had repeatedly instructed her that if she had an accident in a boat she was to stay with the boat, never try to swim for safety in these tidal waters, but she made a decision that today was a time for breaking the rules. She abandoned the remains of *Sharpeshooter* thinking, poor Thomas! His lovely little boat!

Half-swimming and half-carried by the tide she reached the buoy and clung to it desperately looking for a way to climb on to it. Fortunately it had recently been changed from an old-fashioned, towering, solid, slippery structure to a modern lightweight cage over which stiff canvas was stretched. She found she could grasp the bars of the cage and she pulled herself on to the floating platform and waited, shivering, hoping that someone had seen her accident. She would be late back at the restaurant now and she wondered if they could manage without her.

Never mind, she thought. Someone'll come by soon and pick me up.

Then she saw a yacht creeping in across the bar and she realised that with the tide rising nobody might come the long way around the island for some hours.

I might be here all night. Will they remember to fill up the ice-making machine? Did I tell the kitchen about that party of four which is booked for eight o'clock?

And every now and again, as she grew colder and colder, poor Thomas! His lovely little boat! He'll be so upset!

At last she saw, bobbing about far out in the main channel

but definitely, firmly, creeping in towards Barly, a familiar small trawler. When it came close enough she put what felt like her last energies into attracting its attention. At what seemed like the very last minute it changed direction.

"I can't go on pulling you out of the sea like this, my dear," said Abe as he helped Jenny aboard HH241. "You'll have to start being more careful." Then he realised that she was shaking and weeping uncontrollably and he folded her in his arms and half-carried her into the wheelhouse where he wrapped her in a spare sweater and his oilskin jacket. Before he put the engine into gear he radioed the coastguard to send an ambulance down to Barly Quay. Within an hour she was in hospital in Halmouth and both Abe and Thomas sat by her bedside in a little private ward until late in the evening, saying little but each separately wondering what they would do without her. Finally a nurse persuaded them that she really was going to be all right and what she needed now was warmth and rest, so they rode home with Abe on the pillion of Thomas's motorbike. Back in Barly Abe opened a bottle of whisky and Thomas got really drunk for the first time in his life. He was unable to go to work the next day but when they heard about his mother's accident the boatyard were very sympathetic and gave him the rest of the week off to look after her.

After that Jenny only ever put out to sea on Abe's trawler, which she did as often as she could. She felt a lot safer than in a dinghy, even when the sea was rough, and it had the same relaxing effect as sailing. Abe joked that since she would insist on going out in boats he wanted her where he could keep an eye on her.

She liked helping her kindly old friend and became passably knowledgeable about the size of fish they were allowed to catch and the price it would fetch. She still worried about taking the smell of fish to work with her but after a while she ceased to care. She found surprising pleasure in arriving back in Barly on an autumn evening and stoking up Abe's old wood-fired range to cook a meal while Abe and Charlie unloaded their catches, then sitting with them in the warm kitchen sipping whisky until it was time to retire to the Harbour Inn for a couple of pints before closing time.

Realising that the old fellows were no longer likely to be lonely and uncared for, the daughters-in-law stopped coming down to Barly every day out of duty and therefore stayed longer and enjoyed their visits more when they did call in.

Because Jenny left the restaurant on an increasing number of evenings the takings dropped off more than the average for the autumn months. This she ignored, telling herself that she would make a decision soon about the business. She wasn't going to allow financial worries to interfere with the new contentment she had found for herself but she wanted to keep all possible options open until she knew how things would be going for Thomas. He might not like it at the boatyard and taking over the café and the guesthouse might be a sensible alternative for him.

For his part, though, Thomas was as happy as he had ever been, living his dream of being able to spend all his days working on boats. He made the most of every opportunity to learn about new processes as well as traditional methods. His employers liked him because he was careful and capable and he took an interest in the planning as well as the building stages. They sent him to London to help on their Boat Show stand and allowed him to take part in the sea trials of new vessels.

His eye fell on a girl who had come to work in the drawing office of the boatyard soon after he started there. Her name was Sheila and of course she was slim and dark with that particular sort of long wavy hair that he couldn't avoid looking at. She seemd to like him so he took her to the cinema and to discos a few times, that being the sort of evening out that the other young people he worked with seemed to find appropriate. In the summer he brought her back to Barly on many evenings and weekends and took her sailing, which he found much more fun and she didn't complain about. She was more restrained than Maureen had been and seemed to think that kissing and hand holding was enough physical contact.

He knew that it was foolish to continue seeking substitutes for Silver because there never would be one. He tried looking favourably at blondes, or even redheads, and he certainly gave plump girls his consideration, but somehow they never had the same appeal for him. What he didn't understand, as he tried to solve the puzzle of his relationships with girls, was that the stocky, muscular woman with the short greying hair and the weathered face who was his mother had once been slim with willowy legs and long dark hair, and a dreamy look in her eyes.

TWELVE

Thomas never completed his apprenticeship. After the loss of *Sharpeshooter I* he built a Mark II version in his spare time and it did so well in the Sailing Club races during the following summer that everyone else wanted one and the club proposed applying to have it adopted as an official racing class. Thomas knew that he could build them all the boats they wanted if he had a suitable place to work so he turned his mind to organising this.

He made some serious enquiries about the old fish cannery at Innstone. The farmer who owned the land and the buildings, for which he had paid a very small sum of money indeed after the cannery had closed, scratched his head in confusion when Thomas told him he wanted to buy the place. Thomas had called in one evening on his way home and they were standing by his garden gate, looking down the sloping fields towards the estuary.

"Well, I don't know, boy. You see I always did have it in mind to store winter feed there, or house my pigs if I expanded that side of things. But somehow it never happened. Too far away from the main buildings, you see. Needs too much work doing to convert it."

"I should think," said Thomas, "that if you sold the cannery and the river frontage you would have enough capital to build whatever you needed in the right place, exactly to your specifications."

"You're right there. Bit of capital would come in handy. What did you say you were wanting to use it for?"

"Building boats."

"Boats, hum? Rum things boats. I once went in a boat. Took one of them pleasure cruise things up the coast to Halmouth. Couldn't see the sense myself but the wife was keen. Made us both ill. Tell you what, boy, I'll think about it and let you know."

"That's very good of you. Shall I make an appointment to bring a valuer around, just so we're certain of what kind of money we're talking about?"

Once the valuer had named the current price the farmer could expect he was so keen to sell that he became impatient when Thomas delayed to make enquiries about planning permission and bank loans and the cost of conversion, and he even threatened to put it on the open market. But Thomas could not be hurried because he had not yet told Jenny what he was doing, and he needed Jenny's approval because he needed her money.

Thomas set out his proposals in a methodical, businesslike fashion and asked Jenny how much capital she could spare on a long-term loan basis. She knew immediately that this was how things were to work themselves out. She didn't need the business any more and Thomas needed the money. She put her enterprises up for sale and took Thomas to see her bank manager to discuss his proposals and terms for a bridging loan. Then she told Thomas to get on with buying the cannery.

The evening after she had signed all the papers to finalise the sale and to transfer most of the capital to Thomas, she sat in the bar of the Harbour Inn with Abe feling a mixture of elated freedom and morbid misery at having lost all she had worked for over so many years.

"You ain't lost nothing," Abe said. "You just transferred it to where it's most useful. You didn't need all them business worries any more. You passed them on to the shoulders that's ready to bear them."

"Do you think Thomas will make out all right?"

"'Course he will. And you do too or you wouldn't have set him on his way."

"I know he'll need my help and support for a while but I don't intend to interfere. I'll have to keep in the background."

"Quite right, my dear. But you know that won't be enough for you. You got to keep yourself busy. What's your purpose going to be from now on?"

"I don't know," said Jenny. She felt a lump in her throat. Abe had touched on the one thing that had really been hurting her today. A tear plopped into her beer. A big, rough, work-hardened hand closed over hers.

"I suppose you wouldn't be interested in a sort of permanent partnership in an old trawler and its owner?"

The single tear turned into a flood and Abe had no option but to put his arms around her right there in public, so they managed to keep their engagement a secret for no more than five minutes. The celebration that followed became one of the legends of Barly.

The delivery of the double bed on the morning of their wedding day a few weeks later caused a stir amongst the small crowd of well-wishers who had gathered to see them set off for the Registry Office. Most of them had been invited to a luncheon reception at the Harbour Inn after the ceremony but the Registry Office itself was only just large enough to hold the close members of the family, which included the Dogs who felt about as close as family could get although nobody had ever proved a blood relationship. However, none of the Barly people wanted to miss out on anything so as soon as Thomas was seen to leave home to walk round to the lock-up garage and collect the car they paused in their morning's business to watch and comment. They thought Thomas looked very smart in his new suit and remarked what a fine young man he'd turned out to be, a real credit to his mother.

At this point the bed arrived, delivered by a pantechnicon from a large furniture shop in Halmouth and carried into

Jenny's cottage under the surprised gaze of most of the residents of Barly. To be accurate, it was first carried into Abe's cottage, because it had his name and address on the invoice, then it had to be carried out again and into Jenny's, where they had decided to live because it was more comfortable, being larger and having the central heating. Abe was in the process of selling his cottage to a London family as a holiday home.

"What be they going to do with that, I wonder?" questioned one man as the bed finally disappeared inside Jenny's front door. "Surely they got beds to sleep on. It's not as if they was setting up house anew!"

"That one ain't for sleeping, that's certain!" And the speaker laughed loudly at his own wit.

"Oh, but surely! They're not youngsters, are they?"

"Don't know what to do with their money, that's their problem!" Even well-wishers felt a degree of envy towards these two who seemed quite comfortably off and had found middle-aged love as a bonus.

"They say she's rolling in it! Wouldn't believe it would you, to look at her?"

"Can't think of any other reason for him to wed her. She's no Joan Collins and she's got a vicious tongue from all accounts."

On the other side of the crowd could be heard, "She's only marrying him for the security, of course. Can't expect much else from an old fellow like that."

"That trawler must be worth thousands, and there's plenty more stacked away in the bank, I hear."

"Lucky to get him, that's what I say. First chance she's had of a man in years, you know."

"It's her lad I feel sorry for. The one just parking the car now. I heard they're pushing him out. Converting some tumble-down place at Innstone for him!"

Thomas opened the car door for Jenny and Abe to get into the back. They emerged from their respective front doors at the same time, Abe wearing a suit which, while certainly not new, had hardly ever been worn. Jenny had on a navy-blue crimplene two-piece. She hadn't been able to find a hat that looked anything other than silly on her but she had had her hair styled and permed for the occasion and, together with a relaxed and happy smile, this made her look almost pretty again.

Before they got into the car they turned and waved to the onlookers. "See you all soon!" Jenny called. People smiled and waved back and someone called, "God bless you, my dears!"

★ ★ ★

Jonathan Harty meets with Thomas Sharpe and Jenny Baker in a room specially set aside for him at the Marine Hotel. They will, of course, charge him for it and he will pass on the charges in his fees, which he is already certain his clients will not be paying.

"You're perfectly correct," he tells Jenny. "The right to live on the quay and fish from Barly Harbour was granted in 1725, by Royal Charter. It cannot be rescinded other than by a special Act of Parliament, separate from any act taking a waterway out of public use, and the Town Council have neglected to organise such an act."

"Ha! I told you so!" Jenny slaps the table and her eyes gleam with triumph.

"Are you *sure*?" queries Thomas, more cautiously.

"I have had a thorough search made by my office."

"And they couldn't make a mistake?"

Jonathan Harty looks over the top of his spectacles in mock reproof. He is used to this reaction from clients who are in a tough spot and really want thorough reassurance that they need not worry further. "You obviously know little about legal circles in the capital," he smiles. "If my office make a claim to a precedent, the opposition has been known to settle out of court the next day. However, I don't think Box and Baffle are smart enough for that and I won't make any approaches. I don't like the look of the connections between your council officials and certain other parties. I think a lot of smelly fish need a good public airing."

"I'm not worried," says Jenny.

"You don't need to be."

"But there's one more point," Thomas says, still not totally reassured. "You see, Box and Baffle know about this

Royal Charter but they insist it refers to fishermen and my mother's a woman."

"Worry not, young man. I think that in the present climate of law and opinion any court will uphold that anyone engaged in fishing on a regular basis, whatever their sex, must be legally classified as a fisherman."

"But that's only your opinion."

"My opinion, yes. But if the Crown Court finds against us I'm prepared to take it to the Lords."

"You mean I've been in the right all along, don't you?" Jenny exclaims, grinning broadly. "What'll happen then? Will the development have to stop altogether?"

"I think not. But there will be a very considerable and costly delay while they modify their plans so that the harbour and the quay are left as they are, and to make provision for the working of fishing boats. And I think one or two heads might roll in the process."

At last Thomas sits back and smiles. Not because he has felt personally threatened—in the long run the new marina can only improve his business—but because it matters so much to Jenny, whom he loves.

"However," Jonathan Harty cautions, "as I said, all this can only work out in the most advantageous way if we go to court. If the plaintiffs become uneasy and try to settle the matter before the hearing, the results will be less spectacular. So I must caution you not to speak about this conversation in public. Not a word." He glares now at Jenny. His enquiries have been thorough and he knows of her reputation for becoming garrulous when she has been drinking.

"I understand," she says, and she does.

Harty takes out a diary from his breast pocket. "Now, I have the date of the hearing as the 12th October. Does that agree with your information? I shall brief Counsel and we will be down here the day before. Please contact me if you receive any further information, or if you're worried about anything."

"Is there anything else you want me to do?" asks Jenny.

"Just keep on fishing."

★ ★ ★

Thomas had known that it would be hard work organising his business and working on his first few *Sharpeshooters* but he wasn't really prepared for just how difficult it was chasing up plumbers and builders and electricians to work on the conversion, and negotiating the best deals with the suppliers of parts and materials for the boats. He was glad to have Jenny to help him, applying her usual forthright approach to organising recalcitrant workmen and making inefficient suppliers cringe on the other end of the telephone.

It all became a little easier once the work had progressed enough for him to move into his own little flat above the workshop. Although helping him out took her away from Abe and the trawler quite a lot, Jenny enjoyed seeing things come together to his satisfaction and her only worry in life during those months was that he might be working too hard and not eating enough.

It was obvious, though, that as soon as he made his first profits he must employ an assistant to deal with the details while he worked on the boats. In his mind he thought that Sheila would be the person to do this. After he had left the boatyard he visited her sometimes in Halmouth and took her out on the pillion of his bike, bringing her to Innstone a few times to show her how things were going. She seemed interested and impressed and allowed a few passionate kisses on the way home. Thomas attributed her reserve to inexperience and a strict upbringing, and thought he would do the proper thing and let her wait until she was ready. He formulated plans about her coming to work for him and them designing boats together, and eventually marrying.

However, he never thought of discussing these plans with her. If he had he would have discovered that she only worked at the boatyard because, being a girl, she had been unable to get a place in an architect's drawing office. As the boatyard had been told that in order to qualify for government training grants they needed to be seen to be unprejudiced towards women, they had been actively seeking a female to employ and they had taken on Sheila as soon as she applied. But Sheila's intention was to complete her training and then look for a place in a drawing office in London, where she was sure there was good money to be earned and more exciting things to do than potter up and down an estuary in small boats.

Unfortunately she never told Thomas all this. By the time she was ready to leave Halmouth he was in desperate need of an assistant and he offered her a job, clumsily asking her to marry him at the same time. She refused both proposals and they parted with some acrimony, which would have caused Thomas a miserable and lonely winter if he hadn't been too busy to even notice what month of the year it was.

He solved his staff problem by advertising and taking on a jolly blonde girl who loved boats and sailing, and had a degree in business studies. She was brisk and efficient with customers and suppliers alike, and Thomas found he could be friendly with her without the probability of falling in love and possibly offending her or losing her. Her presence took some of the pressure off him and he began to spend his small amount of spare time sketching out designs for the hull of a big wooden cruiser he was dreaming of building one day.

Once he had resigned himself to the loss of Sheila, which he did quite quickly once he realised that the real person inside her was rather less lovable and companionable than he had imagined, Thomas found himself happier even than he had been at the boatyard. Not only were all his dreams coming true about building his own boats. He could see that at last his mother was happy, doing something she really wanted to do with a companion husband who loved her and looked after her and seemed to value her the way she was. He could go over to Barly and see her whenever he wanted, and spend a pleasant evening in the cottage or the Harbour Inn, without having to worry about her any more. He would have liked her to go out in one of his new *Sharpeshooters* with him but she wouldn't. She said she had given up little sailing boats because they were too dangerous.

This state of affairs lasted nearly two years. Then in late autumn, while winching in the nets with Jenny in a heavy sea, Abe had a heart attack.

He had taught Jenny how to handle the boat and haul the nets and sort and pack the fish, but because he never envisaged her being the skipper he had neglected to educate her in emergency procedures, and she knew little that was specific about first aid. So instead of radioing for a lifeboat or a helicopter and keeping Abe alive by resuscitation until he could be picked up, she wrapped him in a blanket in the wheelhouse and took the boat back into Barly single-handed, using the radio to ask for an ambulance to meet them on the quay. He was still alive when they carried him ashore but despite the efforts of the young Innismouth doctor, who also met the boat and travelled with them in the ambulance, he was dead by the time they reached the hospital in Halmouth. The doctor told Jenny it was a blessing really because he would never have been able to go fishing again.

Jenny wasn't impressed with this remark and she told him so. She would rather have had Abe alive to be looked after and loved. She felt she could have managed herself to do enough fishing for both of them herself.

Being young the doctor was not wise and he was not a local man so he didn't understand about Jenny. He gave what he thought was sound medical and social advice to his patient. "Fishing isn't a woman's game. It's a job for young men. It's time for you to settle down. Sell the boat and draw your widow's pension and be thankful you're not in financial need."

Jenny took the necessary examinations for her skipper's certificate and in the spring she repainted the trawler, refurbished it with power winches, and continued in business.

★ ★ ★

After the council elections that May Councillor Box, who had once again been returned to his seat unopposed, became Chairman of the Town Council for the first time. He had been Deputy Chairman for some years and had waited patiently for the Councillor who had occupied the chair for the past twenty-five years to decide that, at eighty, it was time to retire and make way for a younger man. No one in Innismouth and Barly foresaw any momentous changes as a result of his progression because, after all, Councillor Box had as good as been doing the job for the past few years anyway.

During the summer Rufus Black made an extended visit

to the Manor House with his son and a team of architects and surveyors. This team stayed on for some weeks at his expense, causing considerable local speculation as a result of their very professional-looking activities with theodolites and ranging poles and tape measures. The concensus of opinion in the Harbour Inn was that they were something to do with the Ordnance Survey, although there were those who muttered that they were army surveyors in disguise and that a secret underground bunker for use in nuclear war was being planned beneath the hills surrounding Barly.

In the autumn the Black Corporation submitted the first proposed Barly Development plan to the Town Council for discussion.

James Box sold his large and comfortable Victorian house overlooking the sea at the smart end of Innismouth and bought a very imposing residence in a select new development just a little way out of town. It also overlooked the sea, but from a higher vantage point than the last house.

Jenny, always uninterested in politics, never even bothered to vote in the local government elections. Apart from there being no choice of candidate, she couldn't see that the outcome was going to influence her life very much anyway.

THIRTEEN

The Saturday of the Sailing Club regatta produces a cloudy sky and a brisk, gusty, south-westerly wind with occasional showers. The final programme of events has been agreed as follows:

At 1000 hours, when the tide is low, just beginning to flood, there will be an all-class dinghy race around the island, starting and finishing at the Sailing Club.

At 1300 hours the yacht race will begin, out of the estuary, around the fairway buoy and back. At that state of the tide the smaller vessels will be able to slip across the bar safely and so take a short cut out of the estuary, giving them an advantage over the larger, faster yachts. They will all be able to cross the bar on the return leg at about 1500 hours, making an exciting finish as they pass the club house at Barly Beach.

At 1600 hours every boat will dress over all for a parade from Barly Harbour, out across the bar, along Innismouth seafront and back around the island.

The day will finish with a barbecue on Barly Beach starting at 1900 hours, by which time the tide will be at half-ebb and there will be plenty of sand exposed. If the weather deteriorates the barbecue will move into the Sailing Club premises but it is thought that the beach itself is an appropriate venue for an event that will effectively mark its closing to the public.

Thomas has taken a day off from preparing for the Baltic Race. He feels justified in doing this because *Silver* is as ready as she will ever be and his crew need time to rest. In spite of several requests from the Sailing Club Committee, who like the prestige of having the designer of the *Sharpeshooter* amongst their active members, he has no intention of entering *Silver* for the regatta. It would be madness to risk being caught in the scramble of a dozen or so inexperienced and unprofessional crews rounding the fairway buoy and heading for the gap across the bar.

But he does enter the dinghy race, as a matter of business, to show that the new Mark III *Sharpeshooter* can outstrip even the Mark II boats. He takes as his crew the young woman assistant who works in his office. She goes out sailing with him whenever he asks her, which is whenever he is short of a crew member. They win the race with ease, more because of their skill in sailing than because the modification in the design gives the boat more speed. But Thomas knows that the other competitors will imagine the boat sails better only because of the changes and will soon come to him to order the new model. During the race several of the dinghies capsize in the freshening wind as they gybe around the end of the island to come across the bar. A safety boat is in attendance to help them recover, though to some of the spectators it appears that it is trying quite hard to sink them rather than to save them.

After the race Thomas buys a pasty and a can of beer and borrow's Jenny's bicycle, now very rickety and in need of some serious mechanical attention, to ride up to a convenient wall he knows of on the point between Barly and Innismouth, where he can use his powerful binoculars to watch most of the yacht race. His interest is professional on two counts: he likes to see how different boats perform in different conditions and he likes to see how accurately he can assess the total bills for repairs by the end of the race.

The pleasure launches are plying back and forth around the island and up and down the seafront, which seems to be rather foolhardy when there is a race in progress, but the Bakers and the Dogs know what they are doing well enough and the tourists are keen to be immersed in the atmosphere.

As he cycles away from Barly Quay Thomas notices that Jenny and Charlie are very busy decorating their trawlers and stowing pair-trawling gear. He supposes that's to emphasise them as working boats in accordance with Jonathan Harty's instructions. When they are satisfied with their handiwork they fetch pints from the Harbour Inn and take up a vantage point on the harbour wall to watch the start and finish of the race.

Lionel Black has decided that the regatta is a good occasion on which to invite two of his most important business colleagues and their wives down to the Manor for the weekend. They are the leading private investors in the Barly development project and they have been anxiously enquiring about progress for some time. He can combine showing them, in a way that does not allow them to inspect the works too closely, whilst impressing them with his restrained but generous hospitality. Lionel knows better now than to suggest that either he or they join the crew of the Easterly for the race but he would like them all to be aboard for the parade, which will take place under the engine and will be a sedate affair with gin and tonics and pleasant chitchat on board. He even asks Elizabeth if she wants to join them but is not much surprised when she declines. She will watch from the Sailing Club, along with the other wives.

The starting line of the cruiser race presents a very alarming scene with a dozen yachts of various sizes either hove-to and drifting, or cruising back and forth, tacking without warning, trying to get into the most advantageous position for the start. Thomas sees several minor collisions which cause more bad language than damage. Every mishap is followed by a round of cheering from the trippers in the launches, who seem to think that the whole spectacle has been laid on for their benefit. There is an altogether more violent collision between two of the yachts whilst rounding the bell buoy in the middle of the race. They are both going in different directions around it and the arguments as to why, and who was in the wrong, reverberate around the Sailing Club bar all winter. The Easterly doesn't win because Commodore Pritchard miscalculates how near to Innismouth beach they can safely sail at that state of the tide and when the crew member detailed to watch the depth sounder gives him a reading shallower than he expects, he disbelieves the reading and continues on his course. They go gently aground and they have to lower their sails to avoid being blown further onshore, and kedge off, which costs them a good half-hour.

It has never been formally agreed that the commercial boats will lead the parade but somehow, just as the yachts and dinghies are leaving the Sailing Club, all decorated with bunting and ribbons, the launches and trawlers put out from the harbour ahead of them and lead the way around the island and out of the estuary. Being the faster boats, the trawlers steam ahead and by the time they have reached the far end of the main beach, turned, and regained the harbour entrance, flags and ribbons trailing and hooters blaring, the yachts are just circling for their return run. With unaccustomed generosity the launches take their passengers for a final circuit of the island before delivering them back to the harbour. The trawlers come alongside one another, the skippers consulting and apparently passing some refreshments and gear from one to the other. Then, still side by side, they set off across the bar again as though to meet the returning yachts.

As they approach the leading yacht, the big Easterly of course, with Lionel Black and his associates aboard together with the most important members of the Sailing Club, they steam apart, making to pass one on each side of the yachts, well separated so as to give plenty of room. The Commodore and the other members of the crew wave cheerily at the approaching trawlers and Lionel Black joins in, magnanimously, he feels. Too late the Commodore notices that the trawlers are heeling slightly towards one another and, through a haze of *bonhomie* and gin, realises why. Just behind them, and beneath the surface of the water, they drag a pair-trawl net, and by the time he has seen it he can turn to neither right nor left without colliding with one or other of the trawlers.

He shouts to Lionel Black, who is sitting nearest to the controls, to put the engine full astern. Lionel, unfamiliar with the levers, puts it full speed ahead instead.

Spectators see the bows of the yacht lift out of the water slightly, then drop down again as the trawlers are drawn suddenly sideways towards each other and the yacht, the Easterly's speed being sufficient to push her keel over the top of the trawl net. But then the net catches in the propeller and rudder, and as she continues in her forwards way she begins to pull the trawlers backwards. At the same time they heel violently towards each other because of the weight on their net and begin to ship water over their stern quarters. Before either Charlie or Jenny can cut their gear free thay are sinking fast, which they hadn't envisaged, and can only think of abandoning their vessles. The weight of the sinking trawlers slows the Easterly at about the same time as the propeller, still turning, finally becomes inextricably fouled in the trawl net. It continues to churn and thereby to drag the trawlers, decks now awash. The weight of these is too much for the propeller mounting and it rips, shaft and all, out of the stern of the boat, providing a large hole for water to pour into the hull. The bows rise into the air and very gracefully she slides stern first into the water to lie at the bottom of the channel between the two trawlers.

There is pandemonium in the water as the following retinue of boats from the Sailing Club try to pick up struggling and cursing businessmen and club officials, none of whom are wearing life jackets. The rescue is, as usual, made more complicated by the safety boat circling round and throwing lines to people in the water, one of which nearly strangles Commodore Pritchard.

"My God!" cries Thomas who is still at his vantage point on the wall and has watched the whole thing. He jumps to his feet, seeing the flailing bodies and the superstructure of the sunken boats completely blocking the channel. The computer in his brain begins to tot up a bill for salvage.

Two trawlers and a yacht will take some moving and none of the construction barges will be able to get into Barly while they are there.

Then he remembers that his mother and Charlie are in the midst of the mêlée somewhere. He scans the water anxiously through his binoculars and finally sees that they have swum ashore and are sitting on the beach in the wash from the waves, laughing helplessly.

He cycles calmly down to the Harbour Inn, noticing again that the brakes on the bike need attention, and he buys a pint of shandy and sits in the corner of the bar, listening to the uproar of stories being told as spectators pour in. Jenny and Charlie arrive a little later in dry clothes and are cheered and given free drinks. Suddenly they are the heroes of Barly.

As far as Barly and Innismouth are concerned these events completely overshadow the fact that later in the month Thomas and his crew win the Baltic Race, even though they have had a slightly rushed start due to Thomas needing to organise salvage operations before he leaves. They become the most famous names in the yachting world but whilst the glossy magazines are discussing the advantages of the imaginative design and the spectacular result achieved by the way the wooden hull has been laid, and enquiries are pouring into the yard at Innstone, the people of Barly and Innismouth can still only talk about their regatta and the revenge of the Bakers and the Dogs.

The Commodore insists that the attack, as he calls it, on the Easterly was deliberately planned to keep them out of the Baltic Race because of the possibility of them winning, and he decides to bring a court case. But the more he thinks about it the more he wonders how it will look to his yachting friends when he admits to having driven a boat under his command into a trawl net at full speed, particularly as it would seem from the account of eye-witnesses that, amongst all the bunting and ribbons, the trawlers were flying the correct signal flag for pair trawling.

Lionel Black never goes in a boat again in his life.

A few weeks later there is once again a celebration in the bar of the Harbour Inn. Jenny presides in the corner like a queen holding court. She has been there since opening time and has been drinking steadily without having had to buy a drink yet. She is surrounded by a retinue which consists of Charlie Dog, Thomas, Abe's three sons and their wives, Jimmy Dog and, to everyone's surprise, Mrs Sing, whom no one had thought ever drank at all but who is on her fifth port and lemonade without showing any signs of unsteadiness.

To every fresh group of regulars who come into the bar and say "Well done, Jenny! Congratulations!" she is prepared to retell an increasingly embellished version of the courtroom drama, assisted by Charlie and toned down by Thomas who is inclined to interrupt with "Hold on a minute, Mum..." and "He didn't quite say *that*..."

"Just like Perry Mason, she was," Jenny begins.

"Except that she wasn't in a wheelchair..." puts in Victor.

"And she was much prettier," says Charlie. "She had lovely legs."

"She? She? Who do you mean?"

"The lawyer of course," replies Jenny.

"Barrister," Thomas corrects.

"A lady barrister?"

"Yes. You should have seen old Bumblebox's face when my lawyer turns out to be a woman. He didn't like it a bit."

"I thought you had this solicitor from London?"

"Yes. And he brought this lady lawyer to do all the talking. She did it so well, too. Had the treasurer tied up in knots with those dates of the meetings and when things were decided. And then he had to admit that Blacks weren't paying nothing for the use of the council land—the beach and all that."

"Made old Councillor Box look red in the face once or twice..."

"Then she comes up with those Acts of Parliament and those search records..."

"And that historian from Cambridge, the one who's been on telly—where did they get him?"

"Knew all the facts, he did. All about the wars with

France and the south-coast fishing fleets and the way the king wanted to reward them for their help."

"Knew all about a Royal Charter and what it meant . . ."

"And then when he came back—the judge—and gave out all his 'Taking account of's' and 'in the light of's' and 'Furthermores' and 'No case to answer', didn't they all look sick?"

"And the reporters scribbling away and rushing out to get to the phone—you never saw anything like it! I thought for a moment Councillor Box was going to try to rugby tackle them to stop them getting to that phone."

"And do you know," finishes Jenny, "I still didn't understand what it all meant till Mr Harty explained it to us afterwards. Not only can they not throw us out—you should have stayed here too, Charlie—but all development work has to stop pending a public inquiry."

"You mean they might have to put it all back the way it was?"

Thomas says, "It doesn't mean that they won't be able to carry on later. It does mean that it'll have to be done legally and probably Blacks will have to pay a lot more money to the Council for the use of our land."

"They can't put it back," says Mrs Sing. "They can't put back my shop can they?"

Thomas leaves before closing time and rides his motorbike back to Innstone, knowing that Jenny and Charlie will be in the bar to the bitter end and will get very drunk indeed. So he isn't there when they all come out of the pub and Jenny picks up her bicycle from where it was last abandoned beside one of the mooring bollards and begins a triumphal circuit of the harbour, to cheering and clapping from the few remaining onlookers. She rides along the wall, around in a tight turn, back to the quay. She makes a figure of eight in and out of the bollards, around the cottages, back in front of the inn. The bike teeters and wobbles but miraculously she keeps her balance.

"I can't stop!" she shouts. "Ha, ha, ha! I can't stop or I'll fall off and hurt myself! Ha, ha, ha!"

"We'll catch you, Jenny!" shouts Charlie, placing himself

in her path, but she neatly swerves to avoid him, shouting, "No, no, I'll hurt you too!"

I know what I'll do, she thinks. The water'll stop me—that won't hurt. And she rides the bicycle headlong down the launching slipway. Half-way down she sees that the tide is higher than she realised. The water is very deep and very dark. The brakes on the bike are totally ineffective at that speed, and Jenny and bike hurtle straight into twelve feet of moving water which swallows them entirely from the view of the horrified spectators.

EPILOGUE

A young woman post-graduate student of oriental languages at Cambridge, Silver Patel, is intrigued to read in a *Sunday Times* colour supplement about a prize-winning ocean yacht bearing her name. She is even further intrigued when she sees that the yacht was built in a small boatyard near to where she and her mother once spent a summer holiday on an island and she was allowed to live in a tree (she has slept out far and wide on that story).

The following summer she is invited to present a paper at a conference on oriental studies at a distinguished university only a few miles from Halmouth. She decides to extend her visit to the West Country for a few days and make a pilgrimage back to Barly for old times' sake.

She is disappointed to find that the beach and the harbour and the island of which she has vague memories have gone, swallowed up in a thriving complex of holiday flats, leisure centre, and yacht marina. Nothing remains of the old place except the Harbour Inn, and that now has a modern façade that renders it unrecognisable. But she makes enquiries about the yacht *Silver* and is directed the few miles along the road to Sharpe's Boatyard, where she renews her acquaintance with Thomas.

She is sufficiently beguiled by the romance of the situation to agree to be taken on a short cruise aboard *Silver* and to be made love to by Thomas. She finds him an engaging and entertaining companion for a few days but on balance she decides that boats are uncomfortable and not at all to her liking, and as Thomas is obviously interested in little else the novelty of his company soons wanes. He, for his part, cannot understand the attractions of university research and jet travel to distant parts of the world to lecture at conferences and debate matters which, by and large, will have little effect on the way things are done.

They both quickly realise that they have not much in common beyond one enchanted summer in their childhood and they part by mutual consent. A few months later Thomas is married to the jolly, pretty blonde who has been his assistant and crew from soon after the time he started his business, and his best friend ever since his mother died. She becomes a full partner and runs the new repair and chandlery side of the business at the marina in Barly while he designs and supervises the building of the boats at the yard. They are extremely prosperous and very happy. If ever you go to Barly they would be more than pleased to see you.